ALL THAT REMAINS

ALL THAT REMAINS

BY BRUCE BROOKS

SIMON PULSE

New York London Toronto Sydney Singapore

This book is a work of fiction. Any references to historical events, real people, or real locales are used fictitiously. Other names, characters, places, and incidents are the product of the author's imagination, and any resemblance to actual events or locales or persons, living or dead, is entirely coincidental.

First Simon Pulse edition December 2002
Copyright © 2001 by Bruce Brooks

SIMON PULSE
An imprint of Simon & Schuster
Children's Publishing Division
1230 Avenue of the Americas
New York, NY 10020

Also available in an Atheneum Books for Young Readers hardcover edition.

Designed by Sonia Chaghatzbanian
The text of this book was set in Perpetua.

Printed in the United States of America
10 9 8 7 6 5 4 3 2 1

The Library of Congress has cataloged the hardcover edition as follows:
All that remains / Bruce Brooks.—1st ed.
p. cm.
Summary: Three novellas explore the effects of death on young lives.
ISBN 0-689-83351-2
1. Death—Juvenile fiction. 2. Children's stories, American. [1. Death—Fiction. 2. Sports—Fiction.] I. Title.
PZ7.B7913 Al 2001 [Fic]—dc21 00-056912
ISBN 0-689-83442-X (Aladdin pbk.)

ALL THAT REMAINS

1.

ACROSS the table from us Sue sat with her elbows planted on either side of a cup of coffee that must have been cold by then. She held her cheeks in her hands and stared at some petunias in a glazed clay bowl that was the only other thing on the kitchen table. Marie and I held our hands in our laps. The grayish clay bowl was kind of circular but not quite.

"She made that," said Sue, tears threatening in her eyes. "It was her first piece. Oh, God."

"You told us," I said. "At least six times. I don't think you need to make this so maudlin, Sue." This was the first time I had ever used the word *maudlin*. I had missed it on an English test the week before. Dude.

Her eyes flashed at me. "She's *dying*. That's pretty 'maudlin' in itself, isn't it?"

"Yes," I said. "Without any help from you and

six comments about her first inept clay pot."
I had recently learned the word *inept* from
my secret readings of *Tropic of Capricorn*. Well,
certain parts.

Marie said nothing.

"You wouldn't understand," said Sue.

"Because I'm a guy, right?"

"Right," said Sue. "Isn't there a wall around
here you can go throw a tennis ball against and
pretend you're Ken Griffey Jr., or something?"

"Judith's a baseball fan," I reminded her. "*She*
doesn't see it as the ultimate expression of male
grossness." My aunt Judith is one of those adults
who makes no effort to "meet kids on their own
level" and talk down to them or anything. She
and I have watched about fifty baseball games
together on television without saying a word to
each other beyond sharp critiques of the players'
performance.

"Whatever," said Sue.

I was going to go on and tell her that I was
even capable of appreciating tragedy and loss,
but Marie spoke first. "He gets it, Sue," my
cousin said. "Everybody gets it. He's just saying
nobody needs your extra expressions of grief."

"If everybody gets it," said Sue, looking

around the table, again in anger, "then where's her family?"

"We're here," said Marie.

"A couple of pissant cousins."

"Cousins count. Judith has always seemed glad to see us."

Sue snorted but couldn't reply more eloquently. In fact, on *this* visit, our single trip to the bedroom in which Judith was dying upstairs had not exactly been full of cheer on either side. Only her face showed above the light blue blankets, and as she turned it slightly toward us, I thought it looked like a skull half-picked by crows already. Judith seemed to have hung on to only enough flesh to allow her to support these long sores that ran up and down her cheeks and across her forehead. It *is* true there was a kind of quiver in her mouth when Marie marched up and laid her hand where Judith's shoulder might be and said, "Jonny and I are right here." But "glad to see us" seemed to be a stretch.

There was a nurse with Judith, sitting in a slatted chair in the corner like another piece of furniture. Sometime earlier, apparently this person had tactfully but firmly "suggested" that Sue kill time in another room, because Sue's presence seemed to "agitate" the patient and hasten her "deterioration." It must have been hard for Sue to take, the fact that being there with her friend made her friend die faster. But I could understand. Sue's presence would sure make *me* die faster. I like Sue, but she's kind of nervous.

"She deserves more than people just sitting here *waiting*," Sue said. "She—we ought to be *doing* something."

"And you think that if more of the family were here, more action could be taken?" Marie asked calmly.

"Sorry about the 'pissant cousins' bit," said Sue. "But I can't help being mad now about the whole 'outcast' thing."

Indeed, for reasons I had never understood because I was about five back then, when Judith announced to the rest of the family that she was going to move in with her "partner" Sue two states to the north and concentrate on becoming a pottery artist, the adults in the family decided to drop her from the list of people with whom one kept up, and over whom one fretted. Growing up, I never heard her name anymore. We never visited her as a family, though she was the sister of both my father and Marie's mother. Marie and I decided *we* still liked her, mostly because Judith didn't seem to care a cockroach-fart about the family decision, or about much of anything she didn't like. She liked Marie and me, which meant she allowed us to see her live her life.

Then Marie and I went off to boarding school and found ourselves twenty miles from Judith and Sue. We started coming over by bus—Marie was old enough to sign us off campus. Our parents frowned when they found out, but they stopped short of forbidding us. Marie and I both had the feeling we were being watched more carefully when we were home, however, as if our folks wanted to spot any influence, any yen to run off and become pottery artists. Sue was a pretty famous one, with pieces in museums and stuff, and gallery shows. For all her years of enthusiastic practice, however, Judith had never seemed to get any good.

Then all the families had gotten kind of a form letter from Sue announcing that Judith had somehow caught AIDS, a really bad kind, and was dying fast. At the time the letter arrived, Marie and I hadn't visited for a couple of months but we came back right away after getting our letter. We were stunned—Judith was already socked in her bed, looking awfully stickly, and then those sores appeared and wouldn't go away, and although Marie and I came more and more often we couldn't keep up. She was dying faster than we could visit.

We had gotten to know her friend Sue very well in the past couple of years. Once you got over Sue's suspiciousness and crankiness and general air of being afraid that you were going to reject her with cruelty, you could see she was a pretty cool person. She was devoted to Judith, and showed a truly incredible patience with her during the years in which our aunt was making piece after piece of slabby, graceless pottery as Sue was selling amazing pieces to the Guggenheim and Hirschhorn. Then Judith got sick, and Sue was called upon to show a new kind of devotion—which she did well—and a new kind of patience—which she did terribly.

"I know I'm going against the Asian stereotype," she once said. Sue is Japanese, and comes from an evangelical Japanese-Christian family, which booted *her* out, so we've never seen any of *them* around, either. "We're supposed to be stoic and composed, and I'm falling apart."

"Stereotypes rarely apply very deeply," said Marie.

"You can say that again," Sue said.

"Stereotypes rarely apply very deeply," Marie said without a change in her calm tone.

"You mocking me?" snarled Sue.

"No," said Marie. "I was just taking advantage of your invitation, because I thought you needed to hear it again."

"It's a figure of speech," Sue said, angry, "that 'say it again' stuff."

"Sometimes," said Marie.

2.

THE nurse appeared in the kitchen doorway. Sue was rising from her seat and staring at her when the nurse said, "It's over."

"NO!" screamed Sue, and from across the table Marie and I both reached our hands out toward her, though we were in no position to reach her. "No! How could you? I was to be there, I wanted—"

"I beg your pardon," the nurse said, with a little huffiness to which I thought she was entitled, "and assure you that I did not exclude you from the ultimate moment on purpose. The patient was lying with her eyes closed, seemingly asleep. I went to take her pulse, as I do every quarter-hour. I found that she had none. No pulse, I mean. I held a mirror near her nostrils and observed no exhalations." She sighed heavily.

Sue was weeping and kind of lurching across the kitchen floor. By the time I managed just to blink a couple of times, Marie had slid her own chair back from the table and was closing in on her.

"Take me up," said Sue.

"Sure," Marie said, slipping an arm around her shoulders. She looked back at me. "Why don't you make some food?" she said.

3.

In fact I can cook okay for a guy (stereotypes rarely apply deeply). But a look in the refrigerator showed that Sue had been living on coffee and yogurt. Judith, of course, hadn't been living at all, but dying, and it doesn't take much food for that.

I decided to go out, probably for pizza.

It was winter, cold, maybe zero, maybe five below. I walked down the front walk I had shoveled myself three days ago, before the last surprisingly light snow, and I inhaled the cold air deeply. For some reason, instead of seeming funereal or tomblike or anything deathly, the freeze hit me as very enlivening. Enlivening. Somebody was dead, but I was alive. At the end of the walkway I decided not to take the bus into town but to walk to the smaller cluster of shops and bars that Marie and I sometimes passed on the bus back to our school. It was in the other direction from town, so I turned that way.

As I walked I got colder, and began to believe I had overrated this enlivening-air bit. But I kept thinking of pizza—hot strings of cheese as I lifted a steaming triangle and put it on a plate in front of Sue, who couldn't help but be cheered, because who could frown at pizza? These thoughts helped warm me up a little. But when I got to the cluster of shops and bars, I was very disappointed to find that it contained no pizza place.

I should probably say something here about why I did what I did in the next few minutes. I have thought about it a lot since then, trying to figure it out, and eventually this is what I came up with. When you have been in a house where someone has just died, and the death was pretty horrible, part of you looks at the living world as if it must be sort of unified in good cheer. It's almost like, everyone is your friend, because you all recognize that none of you is skeletal and covered with sores and dead; and surely everyone knows this, and good cheer and brotherhood toward all is the result.

Or, to be more blunt, once you have been around death, you don't expect to run into something so incredibly small as meanness.

So I looked and saw a place marked TAVERN and thought that a tavern must have food, so I pushed through the door and found myself in a dark, short hallway, at the end of which was one big room with booths along the far wall, tables in the middle, and a long bar along the wall close to where I stood.

Before I could say a word, a hard-looking man in a white shirt with the sleeves rolled up over tattoos on his forearms looked briefly at me without any expression in his face and said, "Out."

I thought maybe he knew I had come to ask for pizza and was telling me the tavern had used up all its dough or something. "Excuse me?" I said.

"What do you want, I should lose my license letting a kid in here? Beat it before somebody beats you." Now his face took on an expression but it was not a nice one, and he slapped the bar near me with a rolled-up towel that sounded as hard as a nightstick.

I managed to stammer out a reply. "A lady up the street, my aunt, just died," I said, "and I was hoping to buy some food for the people still there in the house, maybe some pizza—"

"The one had the AIDS," said an old man with a bulbous nose standing at the bar midway down, aiming his comment at the bartender, who did not take his hard eyes from my face.

"That the one?" the bartender asked me. I nodded.

"Then clear out extra quick," he said. "Nobody in here wants to catch nothing."

"You don't get AIDS from somebody buying—"

"I don't plan on getting that crap, period," he said, taking another step toward me. A small step. He hit the bar with the towel again. "Beat it."

When you expect brotherhood and get crap like this, you start to get pissed off. But when you're thirteen in a room full of rough guys, you also try to keep your anger quiet.

"How DO they get it?" said another man down the bar to the first guy who had spoken up. "The women, I mean. I know guys, like, mix up their fluids and stuff, but the women—?"

"Who cares?" said the bartender. "It's a judgment on them for being perverts. That's enough for me. And I don't intend to—"

I got madder. I got *very* mad. Shouldn't have, but I did. "Then are you a pervert?" I said.

There was a kind of whoosh through the room, and then silence. All eyes were on the tattooed bartender.

"I must have heard you wrong," he finally said, his voice like rocks.

"No, you didn't. You said AIDS was a judgment delivered to perverts, and since I walked through that door you've acted like you were going to catch it and drop dead any second. So I wondered—would anybody but a pervert be so scared? Seems to me somebody who wasn't a pervert ought to feel safe."

From a booth I saw two men stand up and start to walk toward me. They were hard-looking, too, like the bartender, but unlike him they were coming at me, and unlike him they were smiling.

"We'll take care of him, Duke," said one, without breaking his small smile or taking his eyes off of me. I measured them in my mind's eye quickly: They were each about five nine, one seventy-five, both wearing work clothes and heavy boots. I weighed ninety-seven pounds last time they took our vitals in gym class. I had the feeling the discrepancy would matter now. ("Discrepancy": *To Kill a Mockingbird*.)

Before I really knew it they were within fifteen feet of me and closing, and as I implied, they didn't look like they were going to lighten up on their fun because they were dealing with a kid. So I darted out one hand and grabbed a beer bottle that was sitting on the part of the bar closest to me and, with one motion, holding it by the neck, I smashed it against the rim of the bar. The men paused half a step to take this jive in, but it didn't really slow them much. It didn't even take the smile off their faces.

So I ran the jagged glass across my other palm and started to bleed like crazy. Then I held my palm up and out toward them, the blood running down my arm and beneath the sleeve of my coat.

"How do you know I don't have it too? I'm family. I've been taking care of her. *Touching* her . . ."

They stopped and started to back off, and, feeling cocky, I made my mistake and took an extra step after them. Next thing I knew, something white had flashed out and smacked me in the face like the sprung branch of a winter tree. Something was slung around my feet, and in about three seconds I was outside facedown in the snow, which was probably the best thing for my wound but didn't feel like it. Five minutes later an ambulance pulled up, siren whooping and lights whirling, and two guys wearing rubber suits had me inside and off to the small hospital in the town. I tried to explain that I didn't really have

AIDS, but these guys didn't budge from their suits. At the hospital they hustled me into a special unit, and a doctor looked at me through some glass in a wall. I told him what had happened, and he finally consented to put on several pairs of rubber gloves and two face masks so he could "suture" my hand—twenty-four stitches. After a blood test, I was given the heave-ho and left to walk all the way back to my aunt's house. Crunching up the front walk, I felt as if it had been hours since I had crunched down in the other direction. It had, in fact. Meanwhile, snow had started falling.

I walked toward the light in the kitchen and stepped into the room. Sue and Marie were sitting at the table with a man in a white coat. Sue saw me first and screamed.

"Is your face supposed to be a pizza?" Marie said, frowning and looking worried. Marie never looks worried. Without taking her eyes off my face, in her usual cool voice, she said, "This is Dr. Greystone," indicating the white-coated guy, who nodded soberly at me.

"I thought you went for food," Sue snapped, as I took the fourth seat at the table.

Marie nodded at the bandage on my hand. "What did that?"

"Beer bottle."

She nodded. Then she looked at my face again. "And that huge welt on your face?"

"Wound-up towel, probably wet."

She nodded again.

"Where the hell did you go?" asked Sue. To the doctor she said, "Take a look at his face, will you, see if you can do anything?"

He bent into my face and looked it up and down and shook his head and withdrew several steps.

"I went to a tavern," I said.

"Duke's," Sue said. "Good Christ."

"I thought they might sell me some food—"

"It would have been pissed in if they knew you were bringing it here," she said. "That's Redneck City."

"So I learned."

"Sorry," she said. "Have some coffee."

"Not through these lips, thanks," I said. "In three or four weeks I *may* try an ice cube, but—"

"Your aunt Judith's really dead," Sue interrupted, as if she was finally believing it. "The papers are signed and everything." She paused, then scowled. "What did they say about us at Duke's?"

I thought back. "They wondered how she got it."

Sue snorted. "She got it by experimenting with a *man*."

Dr. Greystone stood up, holding a folder of papers in one hand. He coughed loudly, and said, "I'll be going. If I may be of any service making arrangements—"

"Yes, I'll be calling the undertaker later," said Sue, "though I think there's a lot of legal stuff to go through before you can cremate an AIDS victim."

Dr. Greystone looked fretful. "I imagine there is," he finally said. "In any case—"

He left. No one saw him out.

"Were they going to beat you up at this 'Duke's' or something?" Marie said incredulously. "A *child?*"

"Correction," said Sue. "It looks like they *did* beat him up."

"Not really," I said. "The bartender just snapped me in the face with his towel because I was an idiot and came within his reach."

"But you're thirteen years old and you were coming to get food from a house where your aunt had just died," said Marie. "Why should you have to worry about—"

"You don't understand Duke's," said Sue. She looked at me, dropped her eyes to my bandaged hand, which was completely bound up in gauze and tape as if I were wearing a boxing glove. "They didn't *cut* you, did they? That would surprise me—"

"I cut myself," I said.

"On what?" Marie asked.

"I told you. A beer bottle."

"On purpose?" asked Sue.

"Look," I said, "I'm not really proud of this—"

"What did you do that for?" Marie pressed.

"Two men were going to beat me up," I said. "I broke a bottle and cut myself"—I glanced at Sue as if to apologize for being insensitive—"and told them I might have AIDS like my aunt. I threatened to touch them."

Marie looked shocked and offended, too horrified to say anything except, "Oh, Jonny, how could you!"

But Sue threw her head back and laughed. "Christ, I'm surprised you didn't clear the joint, send them all running out into the snow without their coats, wailing in terror!"

Marie looked back and forth between us as if deciding who was the more disgusting. She decided I was. "Pretending to be HIV positive—"

"He should be okay if he stays away from

infected *men,*" said Sue, bitterness blurring her grasp of biology.

"Well, you can bet on that," I said.

"I would have bet on your aunt."

"How do you know . . .," Marie asked discreetly.

"Because she picked this dude up one weekend—at *Duke's,* no less—when I was in New York at a gallery opening, and a few months later finally told me about it, and I went to the guy's place to beat the crap out of him but he was dead. Need I say of what he died? His landlady told me the whole story. That was about eight months ago."

"And you're still angry," Marie said brilliantly.

She thought for a minute, rotating her coffee cup. She sighed. "They'll probably both burn in hell, but *she* needn't have rushed to join him there." She sighed again. "Do either of you follow the legislature much?"

Talk about changing the subject. We both shook our heads.

Sue said, "Seems like last year they passed a bunch of laws about how people had to 'dispose' of the remains of people who died from this disease. Seems like I remember seeing some protests and stuff. There was something about special graveyards for the 'unclean' and all that. No cremation because it released potentially fatal toxins into the air."

We shook our heads. "Missed it," said Marie.

"Typical fear reaction, of course," said Sue.

"Aunt Judith *wanted* to be cremated," said Marie. "Even before she—caught this disease. She told me once when we happened to be talking in the workshop."

"Yeah, I know." Sue got up, went to the fridge, got a couple of yogurts, washed a couple of spoons, and said, "You better eat what's here and get to bed. I'm going to do the vigil bit. Any objection to staying in your little room?"

This was a small sort of parlor where I slept on a sofa and Marie got a pullout couch. We said it would be fine. Obviously, neither of us wanted to abandon Sue.

We scarfed up the yogurts and went to bed, leaving Sue at the kitchen table, by a cold cup of coffee, looking thoughtful.

4.

THE telephone woke us up. Not the telephone ringing—the telephone receiver being slammed back into its cradle as if thrown from fifty feet. This was followed by a string of words we couldn't hear very well, but which, from the tone, we knew could only be curses from Sue.

We found her in the kitchen.

"That hypocrite of a sawbones could have told me all of it last night," she said when we walked in sleepily.

"She can't be cremated," Marie deduced instantly. "Was that the undertaker?"

"The ghoulish embalmer who preys on dead flesh and mournful souls," said Sue. She went to the fridge and got us two new yogurts for breakfast and poured us cups of coffee. "And that chickenshit legislature that doesn't know an east wind from a viral spore." She pointed at us.

"I am *not* burying your aunt in a leper colony of corpses." She dropped into her seat at the table, muttering.

"People like Aunt Judith *really* have to be buried in a separate place?" asked Marie.

Mocking an effeminate man's voice (presumed to be the undertaker), Sue said, "'The statutes are quite clear and ironbound, Ms. Jo. We are absolutely required to forward all remains of clients whose cause of death was HIV-related to a regional funereal facility administered by the state so that said remains may be interred in specially reserved colonies of plots.' You could hear him licking his lips to get a piece of the regional action, that vampire."

"Is there a time requirement? I mean, within so many hours after death has been certified?" asked Marie.

Sue eyed her suspiciously. "You sure you didn't draft some of this crap in committee or something?"

"Just guessing."

"There is indeed a time requirement. I am to deliver the body within seventy-two hours of certification. The vampire was quick to assure me that his funeral home was certified to receive 'remains' that would then be delivered to the regional facility—it wasn't necessary that I cart the corpse all the way to Kalamazoo or wherever. But if I *didn't* deliver her, the state *would* come for her right away, and then I'd be in trouble."

"Where's Aunt Judith now?" I said.

Sue glanced at me. "In the pottery workshop," she said. "Laid out in a shroud on her workbench."

"What!" said Marie.

"Why not?" said Sue. "I carried her out there myself—she didn't weigh eighty pounds by the end. And it's twenty below outside—she'll stay preserved a lot better than she would upstairs. Plus, telling that nurse person that the 'remains' had been collected let me get rid of *her* at least." She sighed. "But *now* what?"

I had been thinking. "How about a sarcophagus," I said.

Sue and Marie looked at me blankly. I went on. "Didn't the Egyptians used to encase the remains of their special people in, like, hollow statues or something?"

Marie shuddered and looked at me as though I were wacko. But Sue looked interested. "Go on," she said.

"Well, you're a big-time potter, right? You could, like, encase Aunt Judith in clay or something like that, yes? At least keep her sealed off from the other 'lepers' or something."

Everyone was silent, and sat thinking for what seemed like minutes. I was pretty surprised they took my suggestion half-seriously. I was even more surprised when Sue slapped the table, grinned at me, and said, "I think you've got it." But we could both tell she was thinking further ahead.

"Come on, Sue," said Marie. "What is it?"

Sue said, "Let's say you're a state employee working at a regional burial facility that plants corpses of people who died from incredibly infectious and fatal diseases. Now—let's say one of the corpses comes to you in an unusual form, because the deceased happened to be a potter and the friend of a well-known potter, who fashioned a well-sealed, glazed, and hard-fired kind of sarcophagus for her? So that her supposedly toxic remains arrive inside an airtight kind of box fashioned to resemble her form, a box that can still be fit inside a coffin and be buried according to regulations. Are you—as some hourly wage doofus—are you going to crack that sucker open to look inside?"

27

"No way," I said.

"Wait," said Marie, "this is sounding like it might be illegal."

"Then leave the room," said Sue. Marie didn't move. Sue went on. "And suppose that while this human-sized, human-form box was being fired in your twelve-hundred-degree Fahrenheit kiln, an actual human body was accidentally fired, too?"

"Accidentally?" I said.

Sue shrugged. "I store it there and forget."

Marie said, "This could be big trouble for everyone."

"Wouldn't you want some kind of real body to seal inside the clay thing?" I said. "So it, like, rattled or something, if this official gave it a shake?"

"That's a good idea," said Sue, pointing at me. "Would a deer do?"

"I can't believe I'm listening to this," said Marie.

"I think a deer would do just fine," I said, "provided you can dress it. I wouldn't go sticking any hooves in the sarcophagus, in case—"

"No," said Sue, "only a few parts that would be—appropriate to the charade."

"Right."

28

"A poor *deer,*" said Marie.

"You're thinking of Bambi's mother," Sue said to her. "That's because you've never seen the deer around here up close, and also because you've never gone through several seasons of raising gorgeous perennials only to have some brazen deer mosey through your backyard nipping off the heads of every plant and killing them all. Judith and I used to hunt. The woods back there are filthy with deer. It's well known this area has too damn many of them. And let me tell you, they are thick, toothy, graceless things, except when they leap nimbly from the bushes out in front of a car and total it, killing two of the passengers."

"All right, all right," said Marie. "So we can sacrifice a deer. But how do we get it?"

"Well," Sue said, rubbing her chin, "as I said, Judith and I used to hunt."

5.

"**I CAN'T** believe this," Marie whispered, clomping silently ahead of me on her snowshoes, holding the high-tech bow that looked like a weapon from a movie about aliens. "We're actually trying to find a deer to shoot with a bow and arrow."

"We only want to shoot it with the arrow," I clarified. "The thing *I* can't believe is that it was sweet old *Aunt Judith* who used to do the shooting."

"Maybe she talked so seldom because she was mentally lining up another large mammal to kill with her medieval weaponry."

"Or dreaming up another noncircular clay pot to make."

"Don't be cruel," Marie whispered.

"Seems like maybe Judith was racier than we thought. . . . You didn't see Duke's," I said, unconsciously touching the edges of the crimson welt across my face. "Picking up a guy there——"

Some snow fell from a tree branch in front of us and we jumped, to the extent that you can jump in snowshoes. Sue had given us very specific instructions as to where we would be likely to find our deer, and Marie was carrying Judith's bow in both hands so she could cock it——that's right, cock it, because it fired more like a gun than a bow Robin Hood might have used—— and shoot when the moment came. I would have been the one to do the shooting, but my bandaged hand made it impossible. Marie had actually been a pretty good sport about it, once she saw the weird bow. I think the weapon fascinated her, the fact that you could still call such a complex machine a *bow* and zip arrows from it.

"Probably wasn't too difficult," Marie said. "She used to be . . . fairly attractive. Thin and pretty; probably could saunter into a redneck tavern and walk out with a guy in fifteen minutes."

"A decent-looking Labrador retriever could do that at Duke's," I said. "But——would a guy at Duke's have AIDS?" Even my reading of Henry Miller didn't prepare me on the question of rednecks and AIDS.

"Sure, if he was the kind of guy who let lots of women pick him up in taverns," Marie said.

We tromped silently and awkwardly through the snow for a while. Sue had outfitted us for our hunting expedition in a small shed on the back edge of the garden. The larger shed—a true building, really—was the workshop. It stood nearer the house, and she laughed at the way we swung wide of it.

"She's dead, you know," said Sue. "And all wrapped up in linen. You don't need to be afraid."

"Maybe there's a ghost trying to get back into the body," Marie said, surprising me.

"If so, it's having a hell of a time. That body is frozen stiffer than iron. I imagine it's pretty impermeable, even to ghosts." Sue seemed to sense that we might find her remarks about her dearest friend's remains callous, so she added: "That skinny, diseased, burned-out thing bears *no* relation to the human being I knew and loved. You'll feel the same when somebody close to you dies, believe me. All this American reverence for dead bodies is grotesque."

Walking through the snow, Marie and I both hoped we would feel the same detachment from the body of the deer we planned on killing. Marie had already asked Sue what would happen if she only wounded the deer and it ran off. Sue said she would take care of that, then gave us some arrows from a special quiver hanging high on the wall, cautioning us not to touch the bladed tips.

"What's the deal with these?" I asked. "Have they been blessed by a medicine man or something?"

"In a way," said Sue. "They're poisoned."

"Poisoned!" gasped Marie. "But that's—"

"Illegal as hell," Sue said, nodding. "And it makes the meat inedible. But sometimes when we went hunting, especially after losing some of our best plants—well, our purpose was just to thin out the population a little, you might say."

In the end Marie accepted poisoned arrows because she didn't like the idea of making a bad shot and having to chase a wounded, bleeding animal for several miles through the snow. I walked well behind her and kept my eyes on the tips of those arrows, which were strapped to her back.

"Psst!" she suddenly said, dropping slowly to one knee and pointing. I drew even with her and looked. There, across a clearing in the trees, stood three deer calmly eating the branch-ends of a dogwood tree that protruded over the back fence of someone's garden.

Marie loaded up her super-bow carefully and, with great effort, pulled back the thick string.

"Go for the one with the little horns. And remember you've got to hit it *somewhere*," I said helpfully. "Sue said if you miss we've got to chase down the arrow so nobody finds it and kills himself by picking it up by the wrong end."

"Thanks for the tip," Marie said. I watched in awed surprise as she raised the spaceship-bow, sighted through its seemingly infallible paraphernalia, held her breath, and squeezed the release trigger—yes, this bow had a *trigger*. There was a loud *THWONG* sound. Two of the deer leaped backward and vanished. The one with the little horns lifted its head and cocked his ears as if noting the strange sound. Then, after about three seconds, he dropped into the snow and, after kicking his back hooves a couple of times, lay still.

"Jesus," said Marie. "What do they *use?*"

"Awesome shot!" I yelled. I had not seen the arrow fly—it was that fast—but before the deer dropped I had seen it sticking out of the center of the animal's throat, which is exactly where

Sue had told Marie to aim. "I thought you'd graze him in a leg or something."

"Thanks for the confidence," she said. Then she held the bow away from her and looked at it. "Actually, shooting one of these things gives you about as much chance of missing as my Prince racket on one of *your* second serves."

"Now we have to drag him back," I said. Sue was unavailable to help—she was frantically making things out of clay and heating her kiln, all of which she said would take us close to the deadline, after the elapsing of which Mr. Vampire had assured her the "sealed hearse that is really a state vehicle" would call at the house to collect the remains of the unclean dead.

"Boy, *that* should be easy," Marie said, standing up. "A two-hundred-pound deadweight half a mile through five feet of snow." She glanced at me with slight scorn. "And you, incapacitated by your own doing. Here." She handed me the bow. Then she unbuckled the belt that held the arrow case and carefully strapped it around me.

"What are you doing?" I said nervously.

"Well, you have to carry *something*," she said. "I can't try to maneuver that carcass over there while carting poisoned arrows."

35

I accepted the belt, then watched as she walked across the clearing and bent over the dead deer. She looked back over her shoulder. "At least the poisoned tip is still buried in his neck," she said.

"Well, isn't *that* dandy," I said.

"It is," she said, snapping off the rest of the arrow shaft and sticking it in the snow. Then she went to the rear of the carcass, turned her back to it, bent down, and took a rear hoof in each gloved hand. "Otherwise it would keep catching on the brush and things as I drag this thing."

"I'll help."

"Oh, sure."

"I can't believe Sue didn't have some kind of sled we could use," I said.

"She said they always hunted together, and managed to get a kind of sliding momentum going. Frankly, I think they just left a lot of their kill lying where it fell." She grunted as she dug in her snowshoes and shifted her grip. "That's what I hope to do—get it sliding, I mean. There's a good path. You better stay behind me in case I get going fast."

The first few steps seemed almost impossible. Marie strained so hard, I thought the tendons in her neck would snap like overstretched string. It occurred to me that maybe I *could* help. I nudged the thing's head, and its neck straightened out on the snow and came after Marie with a jerk. She nearly fell down face first, but managed to keep the momentum going and, just as she said, in a moment she had him coming behind her on the surface of the snow, which, thanks to some misting early that morning, was kind of icy.

"Going great," I said. She could only grunt in response.

As long as the deer's head and neck pointed straight backward, Marie made pretty good progress sliding him along. But sometimes at a turning in the path the neck would bend, and the head, with those little horns, would catch on something and bring her to a halt. It took me a couple of these dead stops to figure out that I could look ahead, and anticipate this problem, and at just the right moment give the head a kick that would straighten the neck behind the new alignment of the body. I was glad I got to help a *little*.

Marie was determined to keep the momentum going, so she didn't stop, although I could see she was exhausted after five minutes. But somehow she kept it up, leaning forward, pulling steadily, grunting and, at the end, sobbing with the effort. There is a little steep hill at the back of Sue and Judith's garden, and when Marie got the deer over the edge of that hill she let go of its hooves and just stumbled to the side, grabbing on to a tree as the deer slid by itself down the hill and cruised a good twenty feet toward the pottery shed. I tromped over to her in a snowshoe run. She was drooping on a branch of the tree and sobbing with fatigue. Her arms and legs were shaking wildly.

"Drink some water," I said. She nodded. I tilted an insulated canteen against her lips—which was difficult, because even her neck was in a spasm—and she drank a long drink.

Then she said, "Let me shake down. I'm okay. Go tell Sue."

As I approached the pottery workshop building, I suddenly thought that I didn't really want to go inside and see what Sue was doing. So I knocked on the door, hollered, "Deer's out back," turned, and hustled back to Marie. She wasn't shaking as bad anymore. A few seconds later, the workshop door opened and Sue's head poked out. She looked at the deer, looked over at us, and said, "Excellent. Get into the house, I'll dress it right there, you might not want to look." Then she pulled her head back in and shut the door.

We went to the hunting shed, took off our snowshoes, then all of our killing stuff, and left it where it fell, except the poisoned arrows, which we hung back up carefully. Next we did as Sue advised and went back into the house. We sat down at the kitchen table, and Marie ate three yogurts and drank two cups of coffee.

"How does it feel to be an awesome huntress?" I asked.

"Shut up," she said. Then she added, less harshly, "It feels awful."

"The deer probably never—"

"Just shut up," she said. I did.

After a while, during which we heard the workshop door open and close a few times, Marie said, "Why are we doing this?"

"I have no idea," I said. "Must be that Judith said something compelling during that famous talk you had with her about being cremated."

"We were in the workshop," Marie said. "She was firing some pieces in the kiln. This insect, a pretty big one, actually, flew too close to the kiln and kind of—well, I suppose he must have *burned,* but it *looked* like he just turned right into smoke without that step. Then there was a puff of breeze, and he was gone, completely. Judith and I watched as this happened, and when it was over she said she hoped that's how it would be with her when she died." Marie took a sip of coffee and sighed. "She said—well, she said she'd rather be just a free part of the air than be trapped in the ground to turn into rotted meat."

"That's pretty blunt," I said.

"Yeah," said Marie. "So I guess we're helping." She shuddered. "Rotted meat."

"She was already that when she died."

"Well, that kiln will make her a puff of smoke in no time," she said. "There would be kind of a symmetry to the whole thing if she had been any good as a potter, but she sucked."

I had never heard Marie use that verb before, and I just had time to wonder if hunting had coarsened her, before Sue burst into the kitchen and went straight to the coffeepot.

"I heard that," she said. She turned, leaned against the counter, and took a drink. "Judith did not suck as a potter. It's a difficult art, and she was a devoted student." She took another sip and smiled slightly. "A devoted student with fingers of stone and absolutely no sense of design, it is true. But she tried."

She finished her coffee with another long swallow and said, "Do you want to know where we stand right now?"

Both Marie and I said we did.

"Well," said Sue, "I have taken what I need from the deer, buried the rest in the snow for the moment, and sealed the needed parts in a reasonably good-looking, well-sized clay form we are calling our sarcophagus. The kiln is almost hot. In the meantime I am going to put a very heavy sealing glaze on the sarcophagus, a new kind that can be used when the clay is still wet. It isn't pretty—in fact, it's for industrial use—but then, Judith isn't pretty now, either. It's good that I frequently make very large pieces—the kiln is just large enough to accept the form, though how I am to keep it on its 'points' is anybody's guess. I will need your help lifting it. In fact, to keep her cold I have placed her outside, around the back of the building; the kiln makes the studio kind of warm."

"Are you going to—cremate her while you fire the sarcophagus?" asked Marie.

Sue smiled dryly. "That would be pretty poetic, wouldn't it? Not to mention pretty funny. But, no, there isn't room in the kiln. I'll have to fire the glaze—thankfully it's fairly fast to set—and take the sarcophagus out to set." She took a deep breath, held it, and let it out with a *whoosh*. "Then I'll cremate Judith as the form cools." She looked up at the kitchen clock. "We might just make it before the 'state hearse' calls for the remains. Depends on how prompt they are."

Marie and I, not really sure what to do, just sat in the kitchen drinking coffee, occasionally making a new pot, talking about Judith whenever we could think of something. Maybe an hour went by, maybe more. Then Sue opened the back door and said, "I need you now."

My stomach was fluttering when we walked into the workshop, studio, or whatever. It fluttered even more when I saw the body-sized form propped on a couple of supports, glistening all over with stuff that looked like reddish molasses. Sue handed us asbestos things that went over our heads and shoulders and chests with plastic panels to see through, and long asbestos gauntlets. The gauntlets were mitts, so I

42

was able to squeeze my bandaged hand inside one. I wouldn't be able to use it, but at least I wouldn't get burned. Before we put the things on, she said, "Spread your fingers inside the mitts, try not to push through the glaze, watch the heat, lower it as gently as possible but don't get yourselves burned."

"Right," Marie said. Sue went and flipped the lid of the kiln open. I could feel the blast of heat through my suit. We went over to the form. I spread my fingers and put them under the things that stuck up as feet. Marie took the middle, and Sue took the head.

We lifted. It was incredibly heavy, especially on my single arm, and I staggered.

"Steady," Sue said, very muffled. "Get your legs before we try anything near the kiln."

I got myself stable, and we walked the form over. There was a step-up there, so we could all climb up before lowering the heavy thing down into the kiln. The heat was incredible. I guess we lowered the form onto the hundreds of pointed things sticking up like implements of torture, but I don't remember. It was all I could do to get outside and rip off my suit and gloves. Marie was right beside me. The cold never felt so good.

"Back in the house," Sue said behind us. "It isn't healthy to go from such extreme hot to extreme cold, no matter how good it feels. In fact, why don't you try to sleep for a couple of hours? You were up most of the night, and it's evening now. This will take a while to fire properly, or properly enough that we can pass it off on the state ghouls."

We did sleep. I don't know how long it was, but when Sue woke us, it was dark and we were sluggish and disoriented.

"Time to lift the sarcophagus out," she said. "It's all cooked. Won't take a second. Then you can go back to sleep."

We stumbled back out to the studio. Outside, it was cold as blue steel. Before she opened the door, Sue stood there and said, "I have to make sure you're awake enough not to hurt yourself around the kiln. I figure spending ninety seconds out here at twenty below ought to do it."

"Open the damn door," I said.

"Jonny!" said Marie.

"Good enough," said Sue. She opened the door, handed us our asbestos stuff, we put it on, and then again there was that incredible heat that blotted out my memory of lifting the sarcophagus, which felt much lighter now, and putting it, steaming, back on its props. Once more we tore our stuff off, but this time we did it inside the studio.

"I wish I could risk putting it outside," Sue said thoughtfully, looking at the form, but she shook her head. "But even this glaze would probably shatter. I'll cool it in here as long as I can."

There was a pause, then Marie said, "Is Judith next?"

Sue nodded. "While the kiln's good and hot. I can handle her myself. But if you have any last words for her, say them silently. Then try to sleep. By the time I wake you, she'll be cremated as she wanted to be, and we'll have a somewhat strange body to deliver to the state folks."

I was sleepy again. Marie and I made our way back to the room in which we slept, and climbed into our beds. I was just about to drift off when Marie said, "Jonny?"

"Mmmm?"

"*Do* you have any last words for Aunt Judith? I mean, everybody else in the family dropped her. Seems like we ought to come up with something."

"Well, Cuz," I said, "I guess I just thought she was a cool person to have in the family.

45

Nobody did anything the way she did."

"That's pretty much how I feel," Marie said. "And don't call me 'Cuz.'"

Seconds later I was asleep. Once more it seemed as if I slept only a few minutes before something woke me up. This time it was the front doorbell, pealing loudly. A second after it stopped, Sue rushed into the room, looking harried.

"Oh, shit," she said as Marie and I rubbed our faces and tried to focus. "Now I've really screwed up—I should have known better than to sit down in the warmth when I was tired." She rubbed her face hard with both hands, really agitated, confused. "Our time is up. I just moved the sarcophagus out and stood it up against the side of the house, and placed Judith in—"

"You mean those are the state guys?" I asked, looking at the door.

She nodded.

"And what is the problem?" asked Marie. The doorbell rang again.

"Just this. If they—if for some reason they find out what has happened, or if, God forbid, they discover her in the kiln—it *does* take a little while, you know—well, then, I suppose they could take what's left of her."

The doorbell rang a third time. Marie said quickly, "Just tell him you've baked her into the clay form the way Egyptians used to honor their dead, and let him deal with it."

Sue looked at her for a second, then nodded kind of dumbly. She shot out of the room to answer the door. We heard the loud voice of a man who was obviously used to being in charge of things—an irritated man who was trying to hide his irritation and be sensitive to the bereaved—and then the small voice of another. Then we heard Sue's voice, sounding kind of grieved and pitiful.

"Look," said Marie, "they absolutely cannot get a look inside the kiln, that's all. We ought to get out there. If necessary, we can go into diversionary tactics."

I nodded, and ran my fingers through my hair. My bandaged hand throbbed, and I wasn't certain it hadn't started bleeding again. I knew my face looked as if it had ketchup all over it. Plus, I hadn't eaten anything but yogurt for three days now. It was the same with Marie—she had shot a deer, dragged it half a mile, and done that lifting in the studio, all on Dannon fuel. But we collected ourselves for this final effort.

"Ready?" she whispered. I nodded. We went to the door and she pulled it open. We stepped out.

Three heads turned our way and everything stopped while at least two of them registered surprise. There were two men, as we had heard—a big-chested fellow who stood solidly on widely planted feet as if someone were about to try to knock him down, and in his shadow a skinny, nervous little man with eyes that flicked here and there. The big man held a clipboard with a paper on it, a black pen poised above it. He was wearing a plain dark blue uniform beneath an open, dark blue coat, and the bottom edge of the clipboard was resting just above his heavy black leather belt. He scrutinized us with suspicious eyes beneath huge reddish eyebrows, and frowned beneath a mustache that looked like a third eyebrow. I guess the little guy, whose coat was still zipped to his chin, was there to help with the heavy lifting. In his coat pockets we could see large gloves that had been stuffed there. The other man's gloves had been placed finger-end to finger-end and were now carried neatly beneath his arm.

He looked us over and then raised his eyebrows

at Sue. "And these youngsters might be——?"

"Marie and Jon, the . . . niece and nephew of the deceased," she said, naturally enough putting a little extra pathos into her voice. "They have come to represent the family during the last hours."

"Only children for that?" the large man said, raising his eyebrows again. "And stayed a bit past the last hours, haven't they? In any case"——he turned toward us and gave a small bow from the waist——"Captain Hardy," he said. Indicating his beaky helper, he said, "And Mr. Geers. Please accept our condolences for your loss."

"Thank you," said Marie.

"*Captain* Hardy?" I said, my stomach falling. "Are you a policeman?"

"Retired state militia," he said. "First line of defense. Looks like you could have used some defense in a fistfight lately, eh?"

"Hockey puck," I said. "I'm a goalie and I took my mask off too early, to take a drink."

Captain Hardy accepted this and didn't ask about my hand. I guess anything can get wasted if you're a goalie. He went on speaking. "As I was about to say, we represent the state depart-ment of social services slash public health, and

49

are here to collect for special interment the remains of"—his eyes went back to the clipboard—"a Judith Roberts, your aunt, as I understand, deceased three days and therefore by state statute—"

"Yes, we know," Marie said, bowing her head. "She has to leave us now. Thank you for coming to—to collect her."

Captain Hardy looked at her in surprise, then started speaking authoritatively after a moment's hesitation. "Yes, well, sad duty but duty we are —we are glad to execute, as it may be. You're welcome, certainly. Now, if we may—"

Sue said, "She's out this way. If you'll just come through the kitchen—"

"Out?" said Captain Hardy. "Do I understand you to say that the remains are outside?"

"There are some unusual circumstances surrounding this—this body. If I might explain—"

Marie jumped in. "My family is Episcopalian," she said. "*High* Episcopalian. However, following the wishes of our aunt, who was a well-known student of Egyptology, and taking advantage of her friendship with Ms. Jo here, who is a world-renowned pottery artist, we have—the family has asked that my aunt's remains, especially considering the *special conditions* that require the services of you gentlemen, if you know what I mean—well, that, like the ancient Egyptians, in no way counter to our faith, we wrap her remains in what is called a sarcophagus."

During this long speech Captain Hardy's eyebrows had been jumping up and down and on this final odd word they remained up as far as one could imagine them reaching. He said, "A sarca—a sar—"

"A sarcophagus," Sue said. "In this case, as I am a pottery artist with the materials right at hand in my studio, and with an eye toward the possible advantage of *sealing* the remains within a container, not implying anything about the coffins provided by the state, of course, I have made a small, lifelike form out of clay, heavily glazed, to represent the body of the deceased. And it is inside this form that the remains now—rest."

"Now wait a minute," said Captain Hardy. "I'm here to collect a lady's body. And you're saying that instead of that I am to take away a *statue?*"

"Not a statue, exactly," Sue said, looking increasingly ill at ease.

Marie, cool as I have ever seen her, stepped

in again. "More like an encasement. An *airtight* encasement of glazed clay."

"Inside of which the deceased lady has been *baked?*" Captain Hardy said to Marie. He switched his look to Sue. "Or do I have it wrong?"

"You have it essentially correct," Sue said, in a small voice.

"But Ms. Jo has been scrupulous about fashioning her *airtight, watertight* form with dimensions that will easily fit inside any container provided for interment by the state. Our aunt, at the time of her death, was very tiny, weighing about eighty pounds, and thus—"

"I'm afraid this is most unusual," Captain Hardy said. "Isn't it, Geers?" he said, looking behind him.

"Real strange stuff," said Mr. Geers.

"Perhaps you should see the sarcophagus," said Marie. "Perhaps its compactness, its qualities of being heavily glazed so that it is *airtight and watertight* will reassure you."

Captain Hardy regarded her. "Perhaps," he said. He looked at Sue. "If you would be so good as to take me to the—remains?"

We all walked through the kitchen and out the back door. Sue had stood the thing on its feet, leaning against the back of the house. I would have told her standing it was a mistake—somehow, like that it looked too arrogant, as if it were presuming to imitate life or something. It also looked just too weird.

Predictably, Captain Hardy peered at it, then gave the shoulder a rap with his knuckles. There was a slightly hollow *nack* sound.

Sue said, "The glaze is an industrial compound—"

"To be sure," Captain Hardy said, gesturing to Mr. Geers. "If you'll just take the feet, sir?"

In a second they held it horizontally. Captain Hardy took a deep breath, not from exertion but as if for a terrible task, and then waggled the sarcophagus back and forth a few times. Inside, we could hear things moving.

"That's quite enough," he said, nodding at Geers to replace the feet in the snow. He leaned the head back against the house. Then he looked at Sue. "This was—baked in—what do you call it?"

"A kiln," she said. "There, in my studio."

He turned to Marie. "With the approval of the family, in accordance with the wishes of the deceased? *Baked?*"

"As a form of homage, yes, sir," said Marie.

"Also, as my aunt was very sensitive to the nature of her—infectious illness, it was done as a matter of public health. I assure you that, encased as her remains are inside this heavily glazed form—"

"Yes, I see that," said Captain Hardy. He tapped his clipboard with his pen. He looked at Marie. He looked at me. He looked at Sue. "You are aware of the statutes forbidding the cremation of—"

"We are," Marie said, "and to my aunt, who wished for all of the honors attendant upon burial in the earth upon which she lived, this seemed a far safer method of interment."

The Captain looked at her for a long time. Then he mouthed the word *Baked* and shook his head. But he extended his clipboard to Sue and said, "If you'd be so good as to sign here." Quickly, she did.

"Geers?" Captain Hardy said, indicating the feet. Mr. Geers bent and hoisted them as Captain Hardy gently lowered the head of the clay form until it was horizontal.

"Well," he said, "this is most irregular, but seeing as family is represented and public health issues have been taken into account, I see no problem in—"

From the kiln inside Sue's studio came a horrendous *POP*. Hardy, who had taken a step backward so they could carry the sarcophagus around the side of the house to their hearse, stopped. "What was that?" he said suspiciously.

The kiln, as if in answer, gave another, slightly smaller *POP*.

"Air bubbles in a poorly worked piece I'm obviously firing too soon," said Sue. She looked at the ground. "I thought I might dispel my grief by working on some pottery," she said. "But I see my grief only made me sloppy—"

"Surely *this* is pottery work," Captain Hardy said, nodding at the sarcophagus.

"But that—that was for my friend," said Sue. "I needed just to be kind of creative, for myself—"

"And do you think your grief led you to make any—errors in the composition and glazing of *this*—piece?" he asked.

"I can assure you it did not," Sue said, tossing her head high. "This work received the highest concentration one would give to the commission of work by a recently deceased friend."

POP went the kiln.

"Well," said Captain Hardy, "I'm afraid your

creative work is going to be rather a mess. Geers?"

And they carted off the sarcophagus with the deer baked inside, in their state hearse, and we never heard from them again.

POP pop POP went the kiln.

"I *don't* want to know what's causing that," Marie said as we watched the hearse's taillights disappear.

"No problem," said Sue. And we all went back into the kitchen.

6.

"**I WANT** to make one stop on the way back to your school," said Sue. She had taken us out for pizza, then called the headmaster to explain the death in the family, the sudden nature of which had prevented her from calling earlier, and to promise that she was driving us back now that "interment" had taken place.

"Whatever you like," Marie said.

Sue looked at me. "This is a stop for Jonny."

"Me?"

She drove through some back roads and, before I could figure out where we were, she was pulling up across the street from the side of Duke's Tavern.

"Hey," I said. "Look—"

"You just have to open that door when I say," she said, reaching behind her seat and taking out what I could see was a heavy garbage bag knotted at the top. Then she opened her car door and was off toward the tavern.

Marie said, "Isn't this the place——?"

"Yeah. I don't have any idea what she's doing." But I scooted across the seat and ran after Sue.

It was late, and the parking lot was pretty full. "Looks like Duke is doing good trade," Sue said, taking a buck knife out of a sheath on her belt and opening it.

"Sue, look——"

"Really, this is as much for me and Judith as it is for you. You just pull open that door when I tell you, let me do a little something, then run for my car. Okay?"

"Okay," I said begrudgingly.

"Grab the door handle but don't open yet," she said. I took it in my gloved hand. She hefted the black garbage bag until she held it just the way she wanted, then practically all at once she slit it with the knife, jabbed the knife in a shingle beside the door, and said, "NOW!"

I yanked open the door. A wave of putrid stench seemed to punch me in the face like Duke's towel. Sue stepped inside to the near edge of the bar, and hollered, "Hey, everybody—— it's time for a funeral!" Then through the slit she

had made she slung what the bag held in a perfect arc that landed along the bar and slid the
length of it, a horrible slush of blood and guts
and bones and stuff, with one rib taking a beer
glass right out of a customer's rising hand. Then
she pushed me back, kicked the door shut, and
grabbed her knife. She slashed it through the
snow and closed it as she ran for her car.

"What the——"

"I lied," she said as we hopped in the front
seat. "I didn't bury *all* of the deer—only its
hooves. I let the rest kind of ripen in that bag,
near the kiln."

"So they think that stuff is the remains of——"

"Right. Toxic as you can get."

Before we pulled away, Duke's front door
burst open, and we were treated to the sight of
customer after customer rushing coatless out
into the snow to yarf violently.

"I hate rednecks," Sue said, gunning the engine.

"Evidently," said Marie.

"Won't he get the cops to pull us over?" I
asked.

Sue laughed. "Duke is no friend to the police
around here," she said. "There are at least four
brawls there every night, plus he runs a little

numbers racket out of his poolroom."

"If I'd known what was in store for that poor deer I shot——" said Marie.

"It has served us with great honor *twice,*" said Sue. "It has gone straight to deer heaven."

Marie and I looked at each other. Nobody spoke. After a minute, I said, "I'm not sure *that* had anything to do with honor, Sue. Frankly, it seemed pretty crude to me."

"Right," said Marie. "I don't see how it's much different from how they acted with Jonny."

Sue drove on, staring intently at the windshield. Several minutes passed. Then she said, "Okay. Maybe you're right. But it felt like something I had to do, and to tell you the truth, it doesn't feel that bad even now. To *me.*" She paused. "I'm really sorry if that makes me brutal or something. . . ."

Marie and I looked at each other again, then Marie said, "Don't worry about it—we didn't have to feel what you felt."

We didn't talk anymore for the twenty-minute drive back to campus. When we got to the main gate and Sue pulled up to let us out, she said, "Listen, you two—"

"Thanks for taking care of our aunt," Marie said,

leaning over and giving her a kiss on the cheek.

Sue blushed. "Yeah, well. She was my friend." She bent down and looked out at me. "Watch out for your hand. God knows what they did to you in that Podunk hospital—probably left a pipette inside the wound or something."

"I'll go straight to the infirmary." I closed the door. I wouldn't go near the infirmary, and she knew it.

As she put her car in gear, Sue said, "Let me know if you ever want pottery lessons."

"Not bloody likely," Marie said. "I've had enough glazing to last me forever." And in the last sight we ever had of Sue, she was throwing her head back and laughing as her window went up.

PLAYING THE CREEPS

1.

I WAS a little nervous when my mom told me in the waiting room that Uncle Frank wanted, like, to see *me* probably like only *minutes* before he was supposed to die after his heart surgery didn't work. To tell the truth, as I went into his hospital room all I was thinking was, *Don't let him start coughing and gasping while I'm the one in here.* No offense, I always liked Uncle Frank a lot and stuff, but who wants to watch somebody actually *die?*

But he didn't, at least while I was there. He was sitting up in his bed and, except for these weird tubes going into him and a voice that was a little more whispery than usual, he was the same old Uncle Frank, kind of chunky and bald-headed, with these eyes that, I hate to say it, kind of sparkle at you from deep inside these slits that are what he has instead of rounder openings. But it did look like the sparkle might go out any minute. He's my mother's brother and a pretty young guy as far as dying goes, but I guess, like, heart trouble runs on the male side in their family and he had it, and surgery couldn't fix it, so . . .

My dad had died in an accident where he worked building airplanes when I was two or something. I didn't even remember him, and even though Uncle Frank had better sense than to try to, you know, "step in" and "be a father to me," which is a bunch of crap, he *did* always show an interest in some of the stuff I was doing, like by coming to a bunch of my hockey games through the years and even one of my rock-band concerts, though he stood way in the back and didn't stay long. We play pretty loud.

Uncle Frank has a son of his own, just a few months younger than me, and for a long time when we were younger—longer for my mom, because Frank had the sense to give up when he saw it wasn't working—they had tried to kind of force Bobby and me to be "buddies" or something. I guess it was natural we would be put together when Mom and I visited Uncle Frank or they came to see us, seeing as we were the same age and all. But, like, to say the least, Bobby and I were different kinds of guys. Not to be mean about it, but I always thought Bobby was just a dweeb——he liked to read a lot and wanted to talk about his books like I'd read them, too, until he found out that I don't read much; he always wanted to play chess with me; he didn't know *anything* about sports, so if he would, like, watch a game with me he'd ask all these dumb questions about things anybody ought to know. There was some hope when he took up the guitar, but he played *acoustic* and he played, like, *jazz*. I play bass, electric bass, and we just couldn't even start to click. I have to say he was a *nice* guy, Bobby was, never got frustrated or acted superior because I couldn't play chess or jazz or wasn't interested in learning his latest breakthrough on the computer. I was a little less nice, sometimes ragging on him, sometimes a little rough, even, for not knowing stuff about football or ice hockey or for getting his guitar drowned out by my bass at the amplifier's lowest setting or whatever. But he always just took it and smiled and did what he did.

Uncle Frank was more into the things I liked than Bobby was. He never said anything but I could always tell he was a little disappointed Bobby hadn't, like, picked up more from me when we spent time together. In the past couple of years, Bobby and I had been smart enough to stop even trying to find things we could do in common—if they came over, he would read a book or play chess against my mom's computer while I watched the Blackhawks or practiced my bass. When their visit was over and Uncle Frank came downstairs to get Bobby, he always had this slightly hopeful look on his face that went away when he saw we were content to be separate. But like I said, I think really he gave up on the happy-cousins-together-sharing-interests business long ago.

When I went to see him in the hospital, though, that was kind of what he wanted to talk about.

"Hankster," he whispered, shaking my hand pretty weakly, but using my hockey nickname. "Listen, I'm leaving you some dough."

"Hey, Uncle Frank—"

"No, just wanted you to know—it's yours to spend on whatever you want, right now if you like. Or your 'college fund' or whatever. Only a couple of grand—enjoy it. Okay?" I tried to pretend he hadn't said "okay" with sort of a gasp.

"Okay," I said, looking at the floor. "Thanks a lot."

"Enjoy having you as a nephew—coming to

your games, taking you on those travel trips to Minnesota even though your team got its butt kicked—" I laughed a little here, but Frank could only lift his upper lip to smile. My travel hockey team always had to go play a few weekends in Minnesota and we always lost every game to those guys like 12–2—"Oh," he added, "and loved your school grades, too."

And we both tried to laugh. "Anyway—I've got a favor to ask. But nothing to do with my enjoyment of you, or the small amount of money for you to spend. *Nothing.* Okay?"

Uh-oh, I thought, *here comes Bobby,* and I was right. But I said, "Sure, Uncle Frank. What's the favor?"

"If—well, I'm not making any requirements of Bobby, either," he said. "He's my son, and I'm proud of him for what he can do. Good kid. Isn't he a good kid?"

"Sure," I said. "Bobby's a really nice dude, and smarter than anybody." But I knew we were both thinking, *He's just not much of a guy.*

Uncle Frank nodded, as much as the tubes would let him. "Yes, good. I know you two at least *get along* all right, even if your—*interests* are kind of different. Here's the favor: In case

Bobby *does* show any interest in some of the things you're so good at—skateboarding or hockey or whatever—would you lend him a hand, give him a few tips, show him a couple shortcuts? Not to baby-sit him—make that clear. But, if, say, he wants to go ice-skating with you, or needs to know where he should buy a skateboard, or something like that—would you mind helping?"

What could I say? Here the dude's about to die in ten minutes, trying to make it as easy as possible for me to give his son a couple of shots at becoming a real guy and then to back out if I want to—and the kid's my only cousin, at that. "No problem, Uncle Frank," I said. "It'll be a pleasure—like I said, I *like* Bobby. We just never sort of had the same *pursuits* at the same time."

Uncle Frank smiled and looked relieved. "Well, in the remote case that Bobby's *pursuits* change and come a little more into your areas— you'll give him a leg up? Only to the point that it doesn't cut into your own game, or friendships."

I had to hand it to him, he knew how to make it sound minimal. "Like I said, no problem, Uncle Frank."

The sparkle flickered, then came back, but I

could see Uncle Frank was going somewhere deep soon.

He stuck out his hand for a weak shake. "Thanks, Hank. Good guy. You'll have a good life. Do you mind telling the nurse I need another injection? And send my son in, please?"

I left, and told the nurse, and went over to Bobby, who was sitting in the corner crying his head off. I kind of understood. Bobby's mother had died when he was really small, and his dad had always been the only parent he had, so he was obviously taking it pretty hard. "Your dad wants to see you, Bobby," I said, putting a hand on his shoulder. "Dry it up a little, maybe."

He looked up at me, like he was grateful, and right away fought his crying until it was gone, inside ten seconds. I was impressed. He wiped his eyes and stood up. He's almost as tall as I am— and I'm big—though he's about thirty pounds lighter. "Thanks, Hank," he said, in a good strong voice.

"Hey," I said. "Better get in there, though."

He looked at me again, this time with a kind of lost horror in his eyes, then hustled in after the nurse. They both stayed in. Twenty minutes later they both came out, and Bobby was crying again. The nurse told my mom Uncle Frank had died. Just like that.

My mom went to Bobby and hugged him, and he hugged her back gratefully and broke down sobbing. I could see he was actually leaning on her, letting her hold him up almost. There was nothing for me to do. So I kind of gave him a slap on the shoulder, but that was all. Eventually we drove home, and he never stopped sobbing. I thought it was kind of weird, and my mom knew I thought so. Once—we were in the front seat—she put her hand on my knee for a second and said, "It's hard, Hank, being alone."

I looked at Bobby sobbing in the backseat and then looked out the windshield again. "I guess *so*," I said. But frankly it gave me the creeps, and I was glad when I was back in my own room away from Bobby's grief. I watched the third period of a Blackhawks game, pretty much decided that I would spend the money Uncle Frank left me on this Tobias bass I had been playing in the store for six months and maybe a used Marshall bass amp if I had enough left over. Then I went to bed.

Bobby slept in the spare bedroom. I woke up once in the middle of the night and thought I could hear him, still crying. I went back to sleep, thinking through some of the much quicker bass lines the Tobias would let me play in place of my old Fender Jazzbass copy. The bass lines, even in my head, drowned Bobby out, no problem, and I went back to sleep.

2.

BOBBY went back to his house—it really *was* his, now—the next day, all dry and standing brave and straight like he had thought about how he ought to behave as the new master of the household. The household included only Martina, this kind of housekeeper his father had always hired, who was staying on to be the adult around the place. But otherwise, Bobby was alone. For some reason, that's the way he wanted it. My mom invited him to move in with us—seemed to expect it—but Bobby wouldn't go for any of her nice arguments. I vowed to myself I would grit my teeth and visit him soon and often, but I might as well confess that I didn't. My mom pestered me all the time to give him occasional calls at least. I didn't even do that.

About six weeks after Uncle Frank died I got a check for two thousand dollars from some law firm and I cashed it right away and bought the Tobias and the used Marshall, which was practically new and louder than shit. My mom had made some noise about my college savings, but we both knew I very well might not be headed for college unless I got a hockey scholarship somewhere, and I told her what Uncle Frank had said, so she shrugged and let me buy the bass and amp. They used up all but sixty dollars, which I put in the college savings just as, like, a symbol of my possible commitment to higher education.

I was in the basement playing the bass one day a few weeks later when my mother came to the bottom of the stairs and hollered something. I turned down the amp so I could hear her, and she said, "Your cousin Bobby——" but then Bobby showed up right behind her with a brand-new skateboard under his arm and she didn't have to finish her sentence.

"Hi, Hank," Bobby said when we were alone. He took a seat on the only couch in the room.

"What do you say, Bobby?"

"Don't let me stop you," he said, nodding toward the amp.

"No, it's okay, I was just fooling around." I flipped the switch on the amp off, then unslung the bass strap and started to put the instrument carefully in its case.

"New bass?" Bobby said brightly.

Now, I know Bobby, and like I said, he is a very nice kid. I knew he was far too nice to make a reference to the newness of my bass if he was aware I had bought it with money from his dad, especially since he was about to ask me a favor. Some kids are just too honest or whatever to do something kind of sneaky like that, and Bobby is one of them—in fact, he would have rather died than do it if he knew. But still, it reminded *me* of my conversation with Uncle Frank. So I leaned against the amp and nodded at the skateboard he now held kind of awkwardly on his knee.

"Yeah, it's a new bass," I said. "And your board?"

He looked down at it like it was something he had never noticed before, and said, "Oh. Yes. Yes, this is a new skateboard."

I could see from the bottoms of the wheels that he hadn't even ridden it but one or two times yet. I could also see it was a first-class deck with the best trucks and wheels, and probably the best bearings, too. It would be a very fast board. He had probably tried to ride it and fallen on his ass a couple of times.

"Looks like a nice one," I said. "Where'd you get it?"

He named the best shop in the city. Then he said, "Listen, Hank?"

"Yo."

He shifted, and looked at the board again as if it were, like, a weapon. "I kind of tried this out in my driveway? And—well, I must be doing something wrong. Maybe a *lot* of things," he said, and laughed.

I tried to laugh, too. "So you thought maybe we could go skate a little together?"

He looked at me gratefully. "If you wouldn't mind," he said. "I mean, I know it's one of your *hobbies* and I thought if you were going to go, anyway, sometime today—"

A skater hates the word *hobby*—skating is not a *hobby*. It's, like, a way of life. Building little wooden airplanes is a *hobby*. But I didn't bother to explain this to Bobby. "Sure," I said. "Let's go."

"Oh, great! Thanks, Hank," he said. We went upstairs and I grabbed my board by the back door and we went out. I headed for a bank's parking lot I knew would probably be deserted at this time of day. It was level, there were curbs for ollies, but nothing else special about it.

There was only one kid there, a very good skater I kind of knew, but he left as soon as he saw us coming, giving me a nod of greeting. The nod also let me know it was no problem that we were, like, taking over his spot. Some skaters just want to skate by themselves. But this place was nothing special, and he and I both knew he could find a dozen choicer places easy. I nodded back.

"Wasn't he here first?" said Bobby. "Maybe we—"

"It's no big deal," I said. "He was probably going someplace more challenging, anyway."

That made Bobby relax. "Oh. So this is a good place for beginners?"

"Right," I said. Then I dropped my board and warmed up. Maybe I even showed off a little, trying a few ollies and missing, but then starting to get pretty high and landing them over the curb easy. I tried a kick-flip coming off the curb and missed it, but kicked my board upright and swiveled my way back to where Bobby was standing with his board on the ground beside him like a loaf of bread he had dropped.

He was frowning, and looking at my board. "When you try to jump over the curb and don't make it—"

"That's called an 'ollie,'" I said.

"—When you try to make an 'ollie,'" Bobby said, screwing up the verb, "your board kind of crashes into the cement."

I just looked at him. "So?"

He frowned harder. "It must get awfully *scratched*," he said.

I laughed and kicked the back end of my board and caught it, and showed Bobby the underside, which was so dinged up you couldn't even see the original paintwork. "A good skater's board gets that way," I said. "You can't do tricks if you're thinking about keeping a nice finish."

Then I pushed off and showed him a few simple grinds. When I got back I could tell he had probably been gritting his teeth. "Those are 'grinds,'" I said. "That's probably the first trick I'll try to teach you, after we get you riding well."

He looked doubtful. "I'm not sure—"

Oh, shit, he wants to keep his paint job clean, I thought. *I suppose I should at least be glad he isn't wearing a bicycle helmet.* "Okay, never mind, we'll get to those later," I said. "Let's just start with getting you rolling."

He brightened up. "Sounds good," he said.

For the next hour, we tried. But his board

was just too fast—it kept scooting out from under him, and he would fall on his butt, hard. I have to say, he never so much as gave a grunt of complaint—but, man, he took some spills. And as far as skating went—well, it seemed hopeless to me. When a guy can't push three steps without losing his board and busting his tailbone, then I'd say skating is probably not destined to become one of his best *hobbies*.

He wanted to finish strong, though. I thought he'd quit after one of his bad falls, but he waited to quit after his best ride—maybe four steps of pushing without losing his board. Instead of trying to hop up and get both feet on his deck—which he never did—he let the board coast ahead of him against the curb and said, "Well, I think I've learned a lot. Thanks, Hank. I don't want to use up your whole evening. You probably want to get back to your bass." I noticed that when he picked up his board he ran his eye over it quickly for scratches. There couldn't have been many.

We walked home. I skated some as we went, but he kept his board under his arm. He didn't stay for dinner, though Mom pleaded with him, and only as he left did I notice he was walking kind of stiffly—like maybe he had hurt his back during one of those outrageous wipeouts he had just taken.

"Is he okay?" my mom said as we watched him go down the walkway, board under his arm.

"Not as a skater," I said. "He sucks at that—but he never said a word about being hurt or anything."

"He probably wouldn't," my mom said, frowning. "Oh, well. I'm sorry he's not good. You were nice to take him out." She looked at me straight. "You could be nicer if you made an effort to take him out more."

"No problem," I said. Then I went down and played the Tobias. It *is* an awesome bass.

3.

I DIDN'T see Bobby again for a long time. It's not that I forgot about him, exactly. Every time I played the Tobias I remembered Uncle Frank, and his request about giving Bobby a hand. But it seemed to me Uncle Frank had been saying Bobby had to, like, *ask* first, before I could help him do something. Bobby just didn't ask, after the skating session.

In summer I kind of like doing nothing. I sleep late, eat when I want to, watch some games, skate. My only "social" activity is practicing with my band, which consists of only two other guys and me—not exactly a party. But sometimes there is a *real* party, and when everybody has been seeing nobody, parties can be pretty cool.

This girl who's one of my friends called to invite me to a party at her house, and I said I'd come. I even looked forward to it—seeing more of my friends would give me something different to do for at least one night. The girl said it would be a pretty big party, so I figured I'd know a lot of people.

I did. A couple of my hockey friends were there, and I hung with them for a while, and then I went off with some musicians and spent a long time talking tunes with them. My school has a ton of people who play, and they will talk music forever. But then they got into some beer, so I hooked up with some girls who are just buddies and we were standing around laughing about something in some movie we had all seen recently. There was kind of a little disturbance on one side of the room, but we didn't pay any attention to it, until this loudmouth guy named Freddy started hollering out, "We've trapped them all, we've trapped them all, now's our chance! We can clean up the whole school, now's our chance!" A bunch of people were going over to the doorway Freddy was hollering from, so the girls and I kind of went along, too.

I'm pretty tall, so I could see into the room that Freddy was referring to as "the trap." It just took me a second to see what he meant. Inside the room, just sitting around on couches and chairs listening to a CD of this old scratchy woman singer, were six or seven of the guys you might regard as being kind of "effeminate" from school. They were being pretty cool, looking at the doorway with all of the faces staring in, and watching Freddy as he proclaimed the room "a faggot trap—all you got to do is put in some CDs of an old woman singer and you draw them all!"

One of the guys in the room, sitting calmly on a stuffed chair with his legs crossed, was Bobby. And he wasn't exactly out of place.

Somebody called out, "What do you propose we do, Freddy—brand them?"

"I don't know," Freddy said loudly. "Show 'em some good, healthy porno films or something!"

"At least beat the shit out of them," said some other guy from the crowd.

At this point one of the guys inside the room stood up. His name is Calvin. He's a light-skinned black guy, very handsome, and personally I've always thought he had guts, because Calvin makes no bones about himself. He kind of exaggerates the effeminate bit in public all the time, and by doing it he mocks the "normal" guys who overreact and hate that shit.

Calvin is very tall and thin. He was wearing a pale green shirt with about three buttons unbuttoned, and tight, stovepipe blue jeans. He raised his eyebrows at the doorway, and pressed the fingers of one hand against his chest. "Oooh!" he said. "Beating us up! That sounds exciting—think of all that *contact!* But you'd better remember— we feel no manly compunction about kicking you right in the balls if you touch us with any signs of *hostility!*" He lifted up one of his legs and straightened it in front of him, displaying the toe of a patent leather Doc Marten wing tip.

"Ouch!" said some other guy in the crowd, and everybody laughed, and suddenly Freddy's loud thing was a drag, and everybody drifted back to whatever he or she had been doing before Freddy had started yelling.

I kind of watched the door of the room. None of the guys in there came out for a long time, then one by one they slipped out and blended in with some part of the party. Bobby was next to the last—who was Calvin—and I made a point of avoiding my cousin, to the point that I left the party kind of early for me. I was ashamed that I was ashamed, but I was ashamed, you know?

As the days went by I thought about chess versus hockey, computer games versus skateboarding, reading books versus watching baseball. I tried not to draw, like, stereotypical lines. Bobby was a good guy. That ought to be enough. He could do a lot of things, and what he couldn't do, or didn't want to do, he couldn't. So what? I couldn't play chess, could I? So?

But I will confess. Every time I went to a party after that, I avoided Bobby and his friends. I'm not proud of it, but like Bobby, I can't do what I can't do.

4.

THE next time I heard from Bobby was just before school started. He called me on the telephone and asked if I wanted to go ice-skating, during a public skate at a rink that was close to both of our houses. *Oh, THIS ought to be great,* I thought with a sigh. If he couldn't skate on a board, I gave him *no* chance on ice skates. But the rink was one where we probably wouldn't see any of my hockey buddies—hockey guys don't go to public skates, because the ice always sucks within five minutes—and I thought I might as well stretch the tendons a little because tryouts for the travel teams were coming up in a week. So I agreed to meet Bobby at the rink that night.

Much to my surprise, when I got there he was already sitting on a bench next to an old bag that had obviously seen some use. "Do you skate?" I asked hopefully.

"Yeah," he said, "I skate okay." My heart went up.

But then it crashed down as Bobby pulled out his skates. "Bobby," I said, like, incredulous, "those are *figure skates!*"

He looked up at me with his face turning red, then looked back down as he slipped one of them on. "Yeah," he said, "I know. I've always done a different kind of skating than you, which is why my dad and I never bothered mentioning it."

"But—"

"Actually I started skating when I was five," he went on, "so I've had my own skates for a while."

Something felt weird inside me about Bobby thinking he had to keep stuff secret like that. But so I wouldn't think too much about it, I said, "*Five!* You must be awesome!" I hadn't started until I was seven, and I was pretty hot myself.

"I'm okay," Bobby shrugged.

"I'm just glad you have your own skates. Rental skates really wank," I said.

Without a wobble in his ankles Bobby walked to the gate and hit the ice. Well, I had to sit down and get into my own skates—*hockey* skates—and while I did I noticed two things. First of all, Bobby could skate about twice as fast as I could, forward and backward, with twice the flexibility. And second, three of the dudes from my hockey team were out on the ice. One of them nudged one of the others once as Bobby flew by them, crossing over backward—but *with his hands held together behind his back!* And he was wearing *mittens!*

When I got out on the ice Bobby slowed up to skate with me, swiveling effortlessly to go backward and face me so we could "chat." My hockey friends caught up with us and one of them, a pretty mean winger named Dirk, nodded toward Bobby and said, "Introduce us to your *friend,* Hankster."

I said all their names, and told them this was my cousin, Bobby.

"Gee, Bobby," Dirk said, with a smile I knew was dangerous, "you sure skate *pretty.*"

"Yeah," said a center named Pete. "Can you do any, like, *tricks?*" As he said the last word he held his hands up in front of his chest with the wrists bent up, very, like, girly.

As I said before, Bobby isn't stupid. His eyes narrowed a little at Pete, but he said, "Oh, a couple, I guess." And the next thing we knew he was flying away from us with perfect long strides low to the ice, crossing over through one corner and picking up speed, crossing over through the other corner, then heading straight toward the middle of the rink that is reserved for all the little girls in short skirts practicing their little spins and stuff. Bobby was heading toward them going about thirty-five miles per hour when all of a sudden he stuck down one of those saw-toothed toe things and lifted straight off the ice about three and a half feet. In the air he spun three times, then landed perfectly on one skate with his other leg stretched out and his arms out, too, then he went up again right away and spun twice more. He landed the same way, looking as dweeby as could be, but there was no way even Dirk could laugh after that skating.

Bobby stayed stretched out about as short a time as he could, to show the jumps were finished, then whizzed easily back to us, slowed down, swiveled, and gave Pete a shrug.

"Couple tricks like that," he said.

"Very sweet," Pete said weakly, trying to work up some meanness, but he couldn't do it. Bobby shrugged again, then said, "Nice meeting you," and took off. The rest of the time he made three circuits of the rink for every two we made, even when we skated hard, but he never said a word to us.

Dirk and Pete and the other guy, a defenseman named Moe, had plenty to say to *me* about my "sweet cousin" and his "lovely leaps," even though they couldn't say anything directly to Bobby. I did the best I could with their cuts, but when I saw Bobby step off the ice after another half hour, I said, "See you at tryouts," and skated off after him. He was already unlacing his second skate. I sat down and unlaced mine. Without a word we both put our shoes back on and left as fast as we could, stopping at the snack bar to grab drinks. Bobby's cheeks were very pink, so that he looked like some kind of Olympic poster, and I was just as glad Dirk and the boys couldn't see *that,* too.

"Sorry to show off," Bobby said. "And of course I saw what you meant about the— *inappropriateness* of figure skates."

"Listen, Bobby, you skate awesome, and those guys—"

He interrupted me. "I want to try out for your hockey team."

"What?"

He nodded, and finished his drink with a huge swig. "I think I can adapt my skating," he said. "If you won't be embarrassed, I'd like to go

91

over to the rink's shop right now and buy the things I need. If you'd prefer to just make me a list, that would be fine. I'll call you to find out the times for the tryouts. And listen, Hank— even though those guys know I'm your cousin, I'm on my own with this. You don't even need to say 'Hello' once we take the ice at the tryouts."

"Bobby," I said, and I hesitated. I wanted to tell him I was not at all ashamed of him the way he was obviously picking up on. But all I could come out with was, "I'll be happy to go to the shop with you right now. No problem, okay? But—but Bobby, you know nothing about, like, the *game*—"

"There are a thousand videos," he said, "plus, one would think, there are coaches running the tryouts, yes?"

"You can't learn hockey from a video," I said.

"I'm certain you can't. You can't learn a triple axel from a video, either, you know," he said. "But no doubt I'll be able to pick up a few elementary ideas about the game. Let's go."

We went to the shop, and within twenty minutes Bobby was handing over a platinum Visa card to a Midget "A" kid who had fitted him with the very best in skates, shin pads, pants, shoulder pads, elbow pads, gloves, a helmet and face guard, two sticks, and socks and a practice jersey (he chose plain white for both, better than picking, like, a number 19 Red Wings sweater or something, which would make everybody hoot the second he stepped on the ice). Bobby told the kid to pile it all up except the skates which he wanted sharpened now; he would pick the rest up the next day. Fortunately, Dirk and the boys never came into the shop while we were outfitting Bobby.

Bobby took the skates and headed back to the rink. "There's an hour of public skating left," he said. "I'll need all the time I can get to break these in."

"That's true," I said. Then, not really knowing what to say, I asked awkwardly, "Listen, are you doing this because, like, you think your dad would have wanted you to, because he came to some of my games or something? Because, if that's it, he told me—I mean, he was proud of you just—"

"Thank you, Hank, but my father and I understood each other very well," Bobby said, shaking my hand good-bye. "And though I enjoyed those games of yours through the years, the fact is, I'd like to try this all for myself. Okay?"

"Okay," I said, blushing, but he was already through the doors that led to the ice.

5.

I WON'T prolong the suspense. He made the team.

Bobby came to tryouts and outskated everybody, hustled after every puck harder than anybody, and showed a surprising knowledge of stuff like two-line passes and offsides. And though the head coach took one look at Bobby at the first tryout and muttered that he was obviously a "wuss," Bobby worked hard with a couple of assistant coaches and overcame this prejudice. He made the travel team. It was incredible.

His weakness was stickhandling, which you would figure, since he had never before touched a puck on ice with a hockey stick, and no matter how many hours you spend shooting a tennis ball in your basement you cannot come close to what a puck on ice feels like. But he spent every spare second, right through every break, skating around with a puck on his stick blade, getting the feel. Also he had no shot whatsoever, but he had moves, and during a couple of breakaway drills and even once in the final scrimmage he fooled the goalie bad enough that all he had to do was slide the puck behind him into the cage.

Dirk and Pete and Moe kept ragging him, asking him when he was going to do another sweet triple axel, but he ignored them. Once in a scrimmage he poke-checked Pete when Pete was speeding through the neutral zone and would have come in on a breakaway if he'd kept the puck. In another scrimmage, Bobby, playing defenseman, gave Dirk a little hip-check—not a huge hit, but enough of a nudge—so that Dirk, who was coming across the blue line with only Bobby to beat, went down in a sprawl, and Bobby skated the puck to mid-ice and passed neatly to one of his forwards. Otherwise he ignored their taunts.

True to his word, Bobby didn't speak to me as a cousin—only as one guy trying out to another. When the roster was posted, I found him looking at sticks in the shop and said, "Congratulations, Bobby."

"Thanks," he said, shaking my hand. Then he

said, "I don't trust these aluminum sticks, do you? I think I'll stay with the wood."

Our season started. I was a defenseman behind the first line, Bobby was a defenseman behind the third, so his shift always came right before mine. I was too busy concentrating on what I wanted to do to pay much special attention to Bobby. One time he went too deep forcing a kid with the puck wide, and the kid cut back on him and scored, and another time he couldn't cover a huge kid who planted himself in front of the net and held his stick blade on the ice despite Bobby's best attempts to lift it, and the kid tipped in a centering pass from the corner. But otherwise I don't remember seeing him mess up or seeing anybody make a fool of him at all. I remember him just making safe plays out there, clearing rebounds and keeping the other guys from getting easy shots, which is all you can ask of a third-line defenseman. And at every practice he was getting better. He showed that he had good "rink sense"—he knew where he was in relation to the boards, the lines, and the other players pretty well.

Our team went 4–1 in its first five games. Nobody said anything about triple axels anymore.

Then a bad break came. The third line was on the ice, and one of Bobby's forwards made a terrible pass back to him at the point. The puck hit the wall hard about a foot in front of Bobby's knees and caromed right past him toward center ice. An opposing winger had skated hard at Bobby when the pass was made, and now he just kept going in the other direction right past Bobby, who was facing the cage, and picked up the lucky-bounce puck going full speed through the neutral zone. He was a very fast skater. Probably he was on his team's third line only because he wouldn't hit or something like that. Anyway, he was smoking in on our goalie, untouched. Then—I couldn't believe what I was seeing— here came Bobby, head down, belly almost on the ice, streaking in long strides after the kid, who had no idea he was being pursued. In the high slot the kid stopped his strides for a second to deke at the goalie and, because of that, Bobby, with his stick fully extended, poked the puck from behind. He then skated onto it, full speed, made a tight turn through the circle, throwing shavings, and headed—still full speed—up the boards to carry the puck out of the zone.

But, unfortunately for Bobby, a winger for

the other team had slipped his check and was trailing the play, skating all out in the hope of maybe whacking in a quick rebound or even taking a pass from the player Bobby had snuck up on. This winger was coming down the boards straight at Bobby now. They were both speeding as hard as they could go. At the last half-second, Bobby saw him.

Bobby could have left the puck and leaped aside. Or he could have left the puck and gathered himself to meet the hit shoulder to shoulder. But he was still inside their offensive zone, and if he had done either of these things the puck would have stayed inside the zone, too, possibly to be plucked by this winger.

So Bobby slowed for half a second but he gave his attention to firing the puck high off the glass to the winger's side, and out of the zone. This meant the threat was over, but Bobby was completely opened up when the winger hit him dead-on, shoulder to chest. Flying backward, Bobby left his skates completely and started to wheel at just the wrong time. His butt barely touched the ice, and instead he took the full impact of the fall on the back of his helmet. It was the best helmet money could buy, but no kids' hockey helmet could stand such a smack against the ice. Bobby was out cold, and they took him off on a stretcher. A few seconds later from outside we heard the siren of the rink's ambulance as it sped off.

"Aww," said Dirk, "maybe Pretty Boy should have stuck to figure skating."

One of the assistant coaches was standing behind Dirk when he said this, and the coach reached over with both hands, grabbed Dirk's face mask, and snapped his head into the back of the high wooden bench as hard as he could. Dirk kind of slumped down. He was not knocked out, but he was definitely stunned.

"Hey," Moe said, starting to protest. The assistant coach slapped Moe as hard as he could in the side of the helmet. Moe shut up.

"He made the play, you assholes," the assistant coach said through tight lips. "He made the play and took the hit. How many of *you* have guts like that?"

After the game my mom and I rushed to the hospital. Bobby was in a room, asleep, but a doctor told us he had been thoroughly tested.

"Concussion, medium-severe to severe," said the doctor. "He may see double for a month. He may have headaches for six months. He probably won't be able to read for a long time. His folks will have to hire a school-approved tutor to give him oral lessons."

I was in uniform except for my sneakers. "No more ice hockey," I said.

The doctor looked at me with amusement. "Son," he said, "I'll be sending him home on a stretcher in an ambulance because I don't want him riding in a *car*," he said. "No more hockey? No. No more soccer, or football, or baseball, or lacrosse. No more bicycle riding. No more ice-skating, or Rollerblading, or skateboarding. No more of *anything* that could make him fall, or could get him hit by a ball or a stick or a helmet. This boy has a bad head now, son. It will recover. But I will forbid him from doing anything that puts him at risk for another blow like that. Any cranial specialist will tell you the same."

So ended Bobby's hockey career, in a bad smash of small glory during an interleague game we won 3 to 2. His skateboarding career, too—I gave him fifty for his board a couple of weeks later. He didn't want to take the money, even though I knew the board had cost three times that amount, but I made him.

"What *can* he do?" my mom asked when we were still talking to the doctor.

The doctor scratched the back of his own head. "Well," he said, "I guess he could play a musical instrument. A *quiet* one."

6.

"**BUT,** Mom," I said a couple of months later, and it might even have verged on, like, a whine, "I *can't* 'play quietly' with him. He plays an *acoustic* instrument. I play an *electrically amplified* one. And my band—the guitarist in my band plays loud enough to make most people's ears *bleed,* and so does the drummer. We're a shredder-punk band, Mom—we *have* to play loud."

My mother had visited Bobby, and reported that the poor boy indeed had almost nothing to do. But he had discovered he could play his guitar—apparently for hours every day—without pain or boredom. That was about it, for activities.

"Bobby specifically told me he has a new guitar which, while functioning entirely well as an acoustic guitar, can also be plugged into an amplifier to serve as a full electrified instrument. All I'm suggesting is that you let him—he is *so* lonesome—join your band for perhaps a slightly keyed-down 'jam session' or something. It would do him no end of good."

"The guys in my band don't know *how* to play 'down-keyed,'" I said.

"What about the Carstairs's pool party?"

"How do you know about that?"

"Jo Carstairs and I play bridge every Thursday night," she said. "And so I happen to know that your band has been engaged to play for one half hour *at low volume* before Betty Carstairs's pool party. Though why she calls it a 'pool party' in March is beyond me."

"Because it's outdoors. And, listen, the 'low volume' thing is kind of a joke," I said. "I told you, we don't *do* 'low volume.'"

"Your new bass plays loudly?" she said. "On your new amplifier? How nice."

"Mom, that's, like, *shameless*. Even Uncle Frank—"

"One half hour," she said.

So two weeks later, there stood Bobby with my band, The Weasels, on the roofed deck we were using as a stage for our big-time half-hour "gig" at Betty Carstairs's party out in the snow. For the "gig" Bobby had of course brought his famous electroacoustic guitar, and his tiny little Pignose amplifier, out of which, even with the volume turned up to ten, not a note of his guitar could be heard over the highly distorted grunge that came from our real guitarist, a kid we called Meat because he was so skinny. Meat was a typical lead guitarist, which, I should explain, means that he was a special type of asshole. Lead players, as an absolute rule, must be selfish, arrogant, superior, and jealous. They must feel not as if their bandmates are, like, teammates, but rather as if their bandmates are scumbag thieves out to steal the lead player's volume. So the first rule of the lead player is, "Play much louder than anyone else in your band can play." The second rule is, "Play at rhythms you have never rehearsed with them, so they can't keep up, and sound like shit if anyone can even hear them." Meat was a typical lead player, like I said. He ignored Bobby's hand when Bobby tried to shake hands with him, pointing instead to Bobby's guitar and saying, "Your guitar has a hole in it, man."

Three times during the two weeks before we all met on the Carstairs's deck, I had gone over to Bobby's to "jam" with him and try to teach him a couple of our songs. His guitar was this

weird thing made by a company called Ovation—
the front of it looked like an acoustic, but the
back was this curved piece of black polycarbon-
ate that, Bobby assured me, "threw" a loud "cut-
ting" sound assisted by the single pickup embedded invisibly in the bridge or something.

It was quickly apparent Bobby could not
bring himself or his clean-sounding guitar—
from which every note emerged crisp—to play
shredder punk. So we spent our sessions with
me trying to keep up with *him* as he played this
jazz stuff in really weird time signatures, like
15/17 and 6/5. For a couple of hours, it was,
like, not uninteresting to me, once I got kind
of loose about things. And I have to say that
Bobby was the bomb—incredibly fast and clean,
with all these beautiful chords like C 13th
minor-diminished and shit like that, tossed in
with his amazing single-string runs. I usually had
no idea where I was, but he would nod to me to
keep playing, and sometimes he would drop out
and leave me playing solo. Then he would come
back in, following some riff *I* had played, as if
the song were suddenly *my* idea or something.

Busky, our drummer, was nice to Bobby
before the gig started. But Meat just wiped him

out. "Okay," Meat said, before the rest of us were really ready, "we start with 'Fatal Wound' on three, one, two——"

And off he went, sounding kind of like a tuned chain saw, nothing but distortion moving forward in time. Behind him, I saw Bobby, fingers moving neatly at atomic speed, producing nothing that you could come close to hearing. I knew "Fatal Wound" perfectly, but Meat was playing it twice as fast as we had written it. I was starting to catch up, and so was Busky, when Meat's guitar blew.

Later we found out it was just a loose connection between his volume control and his five pickups, which we could have fixed in two minutes with a soldering iron, but at the time there was just this like *BUZZZZZZZ*, and then no chain saw anymore. Meat threw the guitar onto its back onstage, said, "Gig's over," and walked off.

But there was this very small sound of guitar notes coming from somewhere behind all of this, and that's when we remembered Bobby and saw him playing with fierce concentration through his little Pignose. Busky hollered out to him until he stopped, and told him to unplug Meat's guitar and plug the Ovation into Meat's amp, and then to keep playing and we'd pick up with him. So that's what Bobby did—which put his jazzy runs and fancy chords out at an insane level of volume. But it definitely let the audience know that The Weasels were still making music, strange as it might sound compared with what we usually played.

Bobby would play for a while, then stop, and announce the next tune, and turn and tell us the time signature and chord changes, which we couldn't possibly follow. Then off he'd go, not unlike Meat. Busky loved it—I heard him hooting happily behind me as he tried to find the right beat to accompany Bobby's 15/17 stuff. I just played the way I had played during the "practices" Bobby and I had held. Just like at them, he would suddenly lay out and watch me, nodding as if he understood just what I was doing, and then he'd take something I was playing and turn it into a melody with chords and once again off he'd go.

As soon as Meat's guitar had busted, about half the audience had drifted to the back of the Carstairs's huge backyard and started a snowball fight. But the other half had stayed close to the deck/stage, most of them watching Bobby's fingers with their mouths open. They had never seen such playing, I know. What they were used to was something much more, like, brutal, in which the guitarist kind of smashed sounds out of his ax and your primary impression was one of pain. But here was this guy with his fingers flying and you could hear *every note!* It was a whole new concept.

Before we knew it the half hour—actually closer to an hour—was up, and we all suddenly realized how cold we were and so did the people standing around the stage, so we put down our instruments and jumped into the snowball fight. But first I saw Busky go over and surprise Bobby by taking him into this big hug. "You saved our asses, man," Busky said. "And that was some awesome, weird shit you were playing."

"Thanks," Bobby said, as if he weren't quite sure that's what he should say.

I was about ten minutes into the snowball fight before I remembered that of course Bobby with his "bad head" would not have joined Busky and me in throwing—and getting hit by— snowballs. I looked around the deck for him. All I noticed was that his guitar, its case, and his little Pignose were gone.

7.

LATER that week I went to Bobby's house with my bass. The housekeeper answered the door and told me Bobby was in the basement. As I went down the stairs I heard his guitar, wailing away.

He stopped when he saw me, and his eyes went to my bass's gig bag. "Hi," he said.

"Hi," I said. I had not really planned on this— I had just picked up my bass and headed out the door. So I didn't have any kind of speech ready.

"Listen," I said. "I'd like to, you know, keep playing with you. And maybe someday I'll be able to keep up and know what's going on in this music of yours and play a real part in it, but I got to tell you the truth—whatever you're playing leaves me behind."

"It *is* pretty arcane stuff," Bobby said.

"I don't know what that means. But do you,

like, know anything I could learn to play more easily for a while?"

Bobby thought for a minute, and checked out my face to make sure I was serious. "Well," he finally said, "I have been getting very interested in getting into the blues."

I had never played blues. So Bobby told me the changes, which *were* very easy, and even wrote out a bass part to start with. And then we started playing some blues.

It turned out the blues were not uninteresting. And I could, like, handle the basics. As for Bobby, the blues seemed to take him as far as any of his jazz did, but in a completely different way. That was head music. *This* was *feeling* music. But he could still play atomic fast and clean.

I started going over three or four times a week through the rest of spring, into the summer. My mom noticed. "You're playing music with Bobby a lot, aren't you?" she said.

"So?"

"So nothing. I just—has Bobby taken up the kind of music your band plays? I can't help thinking it must give him headaches."

"We don't play that kind of music," I said.

"Oh!" she said. "May I ask what kind of music you *do* play?"

"We play blues."

"Blues!" she said. But that was all she said.

Bobby and I kept playing blues in his basement, exploring all kinds of stuff. Then one day he met me at the door with his guitar case in his hand. "Come on," he said, stepping out and closing the door behind him. "We're going somewhere."

We started walking. After a few minutes I asked him where we were headed.

"The cemetery," he said. His face was kind of grim, and, like, dignified. "It was one year ago today my father died."

Oh. "But why are we carrying our instruments?"

"Because," he said, "we are going to play some blues for my father."

"Bobby," I said, "this is very weird, and, besides, I have only a solid-body bass here. No one can hear it without an amplifier."

He smiled in his grim way. "I have an acoustic instrument, but my father won't be able to hear *it,* either. He's been *dead* for a year, remember?"

Bobby wanted to do this, for some reason, and I was willing to go along. So we walked into the cemetery and found his father's grave, and stood there in the twilight, playing blues on an electroacoustic guitar and a solid-body electric bass that made no real sound except for, like, the occasional buzzing of the low string when I plucked it. We played around with a blues progression for maybe twenty minutes.

Then Bobby stopped playing, and I did, too.

"This sounds like shit, doesn't it?" he asked.

I nodded.

"Let's get out of here," he said, packing up his guitar. "We aren't playing 'the blues.' We're playing 'the creeps.' We left the blues back at my place, above it all." He looked at his father's headstone. "So long, Dad," he said. "I won't be coming back."

"Why not?" I asked, as if I were his father's resentful ghost or something.

"Nothing to do here but play 'the creeps' some more," said Bobby.

So we picked up our cases and headed out along the cemetery road. Back at Bobby's, we played for two straight hours. It was the best we ever played.

As I was leaving, he said, "Hank, I think I want to get an electric guitar and a bigger amp."

"That's probably a good idea," I said. "A lot of

the blues players I listen to on CDs play pure electric."

"Do you think—I mean, would you be willing to help me choose a guitar and amplifier?"

"Sure," I said. I named the city's best guitar shop, and said I'd meet him there on Saturday morning.

He grinned, all excited. Then his face got serious. "Are you certain?" he said. "You're sure you aren't—I mean, some of your music friends might be there, and—"

"I'm not ashamed of you, Bobby, if that's what you mean," I said. "People who get ashamed of people are creeps."

He smiled. "Okay," he said, shaking my hand like always. "Then I'll see you Saturday and we'll buy a bitchin' guitar."

He closed the door and I must have stood there for ten seconds, wondering at what I'd heard Bobby say. Then I wondered what I heard *myself* say. Then I went home.

TEEING UP

PROLOGUE

THE tee plateau of Number 1 was just catching the day's first light on the tips of the grass blades, laying an almost preternatural green glow beneath the feet of the three boys while their bodies stayed in shadow.

"Who's up?" said one.

"I'll wait for the light," said another, "so we can all admire the full beauty of my drive."

"Whatever," said the first. "You, Flipper?"

The light was rising by the second now. The third boy said nothing but pulled his driver out of his bag, a ball and a tee from the pocket of his baggy khakis. He stepped between the markers and bent down. His right arm was almost a foot shorter than his left, and ended in a curled hand that would have fit better on a one-year-old child.

Using this hand as a slight guide on the end of his club's grip, held further down by a left hand that looked unusually strong, the boy took two long, elegant practice swings, peered down the fairway, and stepped up to his ball, placing his feet carefully.

"Hold on," said the first boy. The light now struck high enough to show his sharp face and pale blue eyes. He was staring back, at a shadowy figure moving through the low ground that led up to the plateau.

The boy called Flipper looked up, annoyed. "Jackson, what the—"

"Company," said the second boy, following Jackson's eyes. He was tall, smooth-featured, spoke in a low, patient voice.

"Irons, come on," said Flipper. "You guys are messing me up."

The figure was now climbing the slope toward them. "A female," said Jackson.

"A fourth," said Irons.

"Speaking of 'messing up,'" Jackson said quietly.

The girl walked as if messing anyone up never occurred to her. "Hello," she said as she came into the full light. She was short and thin. Brown eyes, thick blond hair in wild waves. Loose black hockey sweater with BATON ROUGE KINGFISH across the front. Black jeans, small black pack on her back. "You need a fourth," she said. It was not an inquiry.

"The ice rink is two miles west," Jackson said helpfully.

"We play as a threesome," Flipper said with an edge. He bent forward again, dug his feet deeper into his stance, held his club ready, eyes on the ball.

"Not today," the girl said, nodding another greeting only to Jackson and Irons. "Not whenever another player can make a foursome. You know the rules, I'm sure, golf dudes like you. If you got four, got to play four."

"Hey, how about you just play through?" Irons said, holding the girl's eyes and smiling calmly. "We'll wait." He held up a hand to Flipper, who was about to sputter.

The girl sighed and shook her head. "No. You rush your shots when you play alone."

"Try it," Jackson said, pearly eyes shining. "You'll like it. Think of the freedom—as many mulligans as you want, improve your lies, nobody to laugh at bad shots." He made a slight bow. "Not to infer that you make any bad shots."

"You mean 'imply,'" she said evenly. "And I do hit plenty of bad shots, but no mulligans. You boys can hit all of them you like. If I want to improve a lie, I'll do so. Life's too short to hit out of divots." She looked at Flipper for the first time and lifted her chin at him. "Go ahead and hit. I'll go fourth."

"Look—" Jackson started.

"*You* look," she cut him off, and waved a yellow tag with a loop of string on the end. "I paid to play. You didn't. I watched you sneak by the clubhouse, through the woods. I'll do you the favor of showing *my* card if anyone asks us; they do that a lot here." She looked over her shoulder at the sun. "You came early so you could beat the greens-police. You obviously don't know they are hip to that trick. You wouldn't believe how many first-off groups they catch, and escort off the course." She looked at the sun again. "Getting to be less early. You'd better start playing."

The three of them gave a start at the sound of a wood smacking a ball fat. They turned and saw Flipper finishing his follow-through. Without looking at them or his ball, he slung his bag and walked off down the fairway.

"Go ahead," Irons said to the girl. "Don't worry, he'll peek back and get out of the way.

Flipper does this macho thing sometimes. He thinks he needs to compensate."

She looked down the fairway. "He doesn't need to, if he drives like that."

"Please," Jackson said, grandly sweeping an arm forward. "Be our guest."

She walked between them and teed up her ball. Then, as she took her stance, she looked back at both of them. "None of *that* crap," she said. "You are *my* guests." She glanced down the fairway, hollered "FORE!" and hit.

A minute later, after they had all left the tee, Jackson and Flipper realized the girl had not removed her backpack to swing.

1.

"WHAT'S your name?" Irons said. He and the girl had hit drives up the right side of the fairway, and their balls lay within ten yards of each other. The girl's was farther. She set a no-nonsense pace the much taller Irons struggled to match.

"Isabel."

"People call you anything else?"

"Not many people," she said. "I spend a lot of time alone."

"Except on the golf course."

"Where does 'Irons' come from?" she said.

He sighed. "Well. You will have noticed that I am a member of the African-American race."

"I did catch that."

"And I am tall and handsome."

She shrugged at this.

"And of course the prototype for tall, handsome,

African-American golfers with a blistering game is Tiger Woods. My cracker friends back there on the wrong side of the fairway, believing that I fall short of Tiger's game, have dropped me from the honor of 'Woods' to the more commonplace 'Irons.'"

"Pretty clever," she said.

"I don't mind," he said.

Isabel did not ask his real name.

They turned to watch the other two boys hit. Jackson, who had sliced his drive, whacked a hot ball out of the rough, carrying across the fairway and landing beneath a pine tree.

"You got a perfect approach setup!" Irons hollered. "Clean shot to the green!"

"I got a perfect seven setup!" Jackson shouted back. "Wonky shot to the sand trap!"

Flipper hit next. With his left arm carrying his swing from drawback to follow-through, he lofted a short but perfectly straight shot to within twenty yards of the green.

"Flip is consistent. Can bogey every hole. Beats the baggies off J. and me," said Irons.

"Straight and short. That's how my father played," Isabel said. She glanced quickly away. "Your shot," she commanded.

Irons took a four-iron and poled a long, low hook that rolled onto the green.

"Nice shot," Isabel said.

"Sometimes I luck out."

"It's not luck when your first two shots on the first hole are ace," Isabel said, settling over her ball.

"What are you hitting?" said Irons.

She ignored him and struck a high, long, right-to-left shot that plopped on the back third of the green, kept rolling, and dipped off the edge of the green out of sight.

"Oops," said Irons. "On the beach."

Putting her club back in the bag, Isabel nodded and said, "I brought sunscreen and my belly-board."

"Maybe you should try it without a pack on your back," Irons said as they resumed walking. "You may have noticed most golfers play without such items. Is it, like, a personal handicap or something?"

"Something," she said.

"I wouldn't dare ask what's inside."

"No," she said, looking at him, "you wouldn't."

As they walked, Irons said, "So you say your father played?"

Head down beside him, she ignored the question.

"He teach you?"

She hesitated, frowning. She finally said, "What I know I learned from him, yes."

"Lessons, too?"

She looked up at him, angry. "I said I learned what I know from my father."

He held up his hands. "Hey, sorry. Next time I'll listen with immaculate comprehension, okay?"

She looked ahead. "Suit yourself. If there's anything to listen to."

Irons waited a moment, then said, more softly, "You spoke of him in the past tense."

"Did I?" They stopped in silence as Jackson topped the ball weakly out of the rough on the other side, after which Flipper pitched neatly to within ten feet of the cup.

Isabel started walking away from Irons before Flipper's ball had stopped rolling. The boys watched her vanish downhill over the back edge of the green.

Jackson chipped to the middle of the green. As the threesome stepped onto the putting surface, a ball rose with a nimbus of sand from the back. It landed, rolled down the green's slope, and stopped seven feet beneath the hole.

"Not a bad blast," said Jackson.

"Especially with a *seven*," Irons said, in a half-whisper.

The other two gaped at him. He went on, watching Isabel come over the crest. "She carries only three clubs and a putter, none of them matched. A three-wood, a three-iron, a seven-iron. Not much to work with."

Flipper smirked. "Probably ripped them off outside the clubhouse, one by one."

Irons shook his head. Jackson said, "She also carries a backpack. I mean, she *swings* with a backpack. What's *that* about?"

Isabel was standing by her ball. She said, "You're away, Jackson."

"Not for long," Jackson said cheerily, stepping up to his ball and thwacking it to within three feet of the cup.

"That's a gimme," said Irons. Jackson picked up.

Isabel was next. She looked over the line of her putt from behind the ball, then stepped over it and took a few practice strokes. Flipper made an impatient movement. Without looking up, Isabel said, "Get some manners, Speedy."

Then she stroked her putt. She had misread the break, and left the ball five feet above the hole.

"Gimme," Flipper said, moving to his ball.

Isabel calmly marked her ball.

"I said, 'Gimme,'" Flipper snapped. "We don't want to be here all morning while you mess around with your putter."

"Did you ever think about the weird nature of golf?" she said, looking him in the eye. "I mean, you—well, not you *personally*—you pay money to go out on carefully designed pieces of grass and hit shots. One would suppose that hitting shots was *fun,* right? But the purpose is to hit as *few* shots as possible." She smiled slightly. Flipper did not respond. "So," she went on, "I want at least to take all the shots I must. Shots are the *point* for me—I'm not good enough yet to worry about my score." She pointed to Flipper's ball. "You're up."

They finished the hole. Flipper and Irons tied.

2.

ALL of them made six on the second hole, a short par four. Jackson saved his double-bogey by sinking a straight twenty-two-foot putt. Flipper snorted, Irons and Isabel said, "Nice," Jackson himself hooted.

On the third hole, a par three with water in front of the green, Jackson flew long, into some scrub oaks. He just managed to say, "Hey, at least I stayed dry," before Flipper hit a high, straight ball that plopped into the pond, fifteen feet short of the edge of the grass. He cursed bitterly and muttered, "Not enough club."

"Not enough arms," said Jackson. Flipper coughed out a laugh.

Irons's ball was a little low, but held the back of the green. Isabel stepped up.

"What are you hitting?" said Flipper. "I'd suggest a five or a six."

Looking at the green, Isabel said, "You know what? I bet you are perfectly aware I don't have either." She swung hard, grunting as her seven-iron popped the ball high and long. Just long enough—it landed above the hole with good backspin and tucked to within five feet.

"Tight!" Jackson said, sounding genuinely pleased.

"You the *man!*" said Irons.

"I'll hit again from here," said Flipper.

Irons whispered to Isabel, "Taking a drop is admitting a goof."

If Flipper heard, he ignored it, and—using a longer club—arched his ball pin-high, eighteen feet to the left of the cup.

"Good one, Flip," said Irons.

"Yeah," said Jackson with a wicked smile. "Dynamite *third* shot." He whispered to Isabel, "Sometimes he 'forgets' to count the wet ball as two strokes."

Flipper, who understood the gibe, flipped them off as he led the way toward the small bridge that crossed the water to the green.

This time Isabel found herself walking with Jackson.

"Come here often?" he said.

"Oh yeah," she said. "The frozen margaritas are just awesome, and I meet the greatest guys."

He laughed. "Me, I find their microbrewed cedar-aged Autumn Bock Pale Wheat Ale to be among the top thirty I have ever tasted. And, of course, the chicks are convenient."

He waited for her to keep up the joke. She didn't. He said, "So, what's in the pack?"

"My privacy," she said.

"Oooh," he said, "that's pretty heavy. But, see, there's no privacy allowed in a foursome."

She glanced at him with raised eyebrows. "Apparently not."

They arrived at the green and dispersed to their balls. The scores ran five, four, three, two—Jackson, Irons, Flipper, Isabel.

"I know what's in the mystery pack," Irons said after Isabel holed her putt. "A fairly large lucky charm."

"She needs it," Flipper said, turning away with his three.

"I don't think so," Jackson said, smiling with his five.

3.

IT was only a matter of time until Isabel and Flipper landed their drives in the same area and had to walk up the fairway together. It happened on the seventh hole, a par five, when Irons and Jackson hit duck hooks into the left rough while she and Flipper drove straight and long up the right side.

It surprised Isabel that Flipper did not scurry away and leave her to walk alone but hesitated for a couple of strides to let her catch up to him. He didn't actually look at her, and she didn't actually speak. But in a technical sense, they walked together, and slowly. Jackson and Irons would be a while finding where their shots had wound up, then trying to wrench the balls from the long rough.

"Well," Flipper said suddenly, "aren't you going to say it?"

"Say what?"

He barked a bitter laugh and spoke in a sarcastic, high voice. "It's just amazing a one-armed boy can play golf! How on earth do you manage to do it?"

"It never occurred to me to say it," said Isabel.

He looked at her narrowly. "Then you're the first," he said. "What a relief."

"I don't think you're relieved, actually," Isabel said, looking at him. "I think you're disappointed."

"You *jerk,* you can't—"

Isabel spoke over him. "And you're not one-armed. You're not even one-handed. Why say you're worse off than you are, unless you're looking for pity or admiration or both?"

It seemed Flipper did not know how to react. He burned while they stopped to watch Irons and Jackson hack bloopers into the fairway. Then Flipper looked at Isabel for a long moment. He sighed and said, "Okay. *Okay?*" He waited. After a second, Isabel gave a nod. "Now," he went on. "If *I* can take all that, then *you* can tell me what's in the pack and why you wear it like a spine deformity."

Before she could hesitate, Isabel made herself

say, "It's a thick cardboard box with my father's ashes in it. He was cremated almost a month ago."

Flipper's eyes bugged. "His—like, what his body was turned into?"

She said, "His bones, mostly, plus some pine ash from the cheap coffin he was in." For the first time that day, Isabel looked as if she wanted to say more but was not sure what it should be.

Flipper, still looking amazed, saved her the trouble. "And have you been carrying his ashes the whole time?"

"Not *all* the time." She sighed. "But whenever I play, yes."

They turned at the sound of a skulled iron shot, and watched Jackson put his hand as a brim over his eyes, looking high over the fairway while his ball rolled no more than thirty yards. Irons laughed at the gesture, then hit a decent three-wood that took him to within a wedge shot of the green. He bowed toward Flipper and Isabel, who applauded briefly.

Jackson finally hit a good shot, too.

Flipper and Isabel resumed their walk. "So he just died? A month ago or something?"

"Right," she said.

Flipper hesitated. "How?"

She took a deep breath. "Well—a drug over-dose."

Flipper gaped, nearly stopped walking, then fought the expression off his face and kept moving. "Wow. I mean—I'm sorry."

"Okay, thanks," she said. She walked up and glanced at the balls. Hers was farther from the green. "I'm away." She took out her three-iron, looking up the fairway, and hit a long, low shot that followed the distant dogleg left. Without a word, Flipper stepped up to his ball and lofted a shorter shot with his usual straightness.

"Speaking of playing well," he said, "you hit great."

"Thanks," Isabel said. They started walking again, pausing whenever Irons or Jackson hit, still straggling along across the fairway.

"I guess I'd like to know how you learned," Flipper said after a few steps.

"My father played all the time. He brought me along, and taught me. He was a great teacher. That's how I learned."

She looked over at him with a small smile. "Your turn."

"Okay," he said. He thought for a minute as they came up to his ball. He looked at her and smiled quickly. "But when I talk about stuff, sometimes I get pretty hostile. You probably noticed?"

"Hostile is okay," she said.

"I guess it's obvious I was born like this," he said, casually flapping his short arm. "I mean, one of your arms doesn't suddenly just shrivel one day. Skip the technical stuff, but I could always move everything well enough to do without any stupid fake 'normalcy aids.' I should say, I could do everything except the right sport."

"What about football?" Isabel said. "You could be an offensive lineman. What about soccer? It's all feet."

"Hate 'em both," said Flipper. "Too *easy*."

"Ah," she said. "I think I got it."

"Yeah," he said. "Boy-with-withered-arm had to play the hardest game there was for him."

Isabel nodded. "But how——"

Flipper gestured over the fairway toward Irons and Jackson. "Those two guys. They, like, mocked me, bet me I couldn't swing a club, hit a ball, make a putt—after a few months I saw they weren't really mocking. They were, like, teaching me by challenging me. With no special treatment."

"Right," she said. "Calling you 'Flipper.'"

He blushed. "Don't tell them," he said, "but I love that."

"I think they know," she said.

He shrugged.

Then he stepped up and sliced deep into the trees on the right. They walked different ways. As it happened, the three boys—taking several more shots each than Isabel reached the green ahead of her, because her long approach was accurate but too hot. The ball bounded over the edge of a sand trap to the far edge of a small stream that trickled thirty yards past the hole.

The boys waited, whispering together, while Isabel considered her shot.

Her ball rested on shafts of long grass that grew downward toward the water; if she stepped near it, or set her club, she would dislodge it into the drink. She had to chop down, with her feet above the ball, and scoop under it enough to clear the bunker. Yet the shot needed backspin to bite the green immediately, which meant a lot of loft. All this in a few yards.

Holding her seven-iron down the shaft, leading the downswing with her hands, she spooned the ball off the grass with a clean flick, laying the blade of the iron flat as if it were a pitching wedge. Isabel looked up a split second after hitting, and watched the ball arc up, peak sharply, drop onto the green, and roll nicely to within three feet of the cup. Then she made to leap the creek.

"Not bad, Ashes," said Jackson.

She looked up sharply, not even noticing that one foot landed in the water. "Damn you," she said to Flipper, who cowed a little.

"Not his fault," said Irons. "I told you—no privacy in a foursome. We threatened to twist his nubbin unless he told us all."

"He wouldn't have minded much," Jackson said. "We suspect it's really his G-spot."

But Flipper looked as if he minded the immediate openness quite a bit. Isabel looked as if she minded it more. She walked over, picked up her ball, and headed for the next tee without a word.

The boys, too, were quiet as they putted out. Only Jackson spoke. "I knew she would take a 'gimme' sooner or later," he said.

4.

AT the break after the first nine holes, Irons, Jackson, and Flipper sat at a picnic table drinking sodas from a machine outside the clubhouse. Isabel did not join them. She sat forty feet away beneath a tree, with a bottle of water taken from her golf bag. No one spoke to her on the tenth tee, but when she and Irons drove close together into the tangled rough along the fairway of the par four, Irons would not leave her to walk alone.

"I hate to be preachy and explain the obvious," he said to her stony profile, "but you must know we give each other a hard time because we're friends. We all know a lot of things about each other, a lot of bad things. Sad things. We're crude, but we're not jerks. It cuts us up, hearing about your father. Maybe we want to help if we can."

"Then just leave me alone," she said harshly.

"Well," Irons said, "I don't think that would be any way to help much. We figure you must have decided to do whatever people with ashes do—'scatter them,' I guess—somewhere on the golf course. But you've been bringing them out here for weeks in that pack. Why haven't you done the deed? I bet it's because even though you won't play alone, as you told us, you keep your secret and never loosen up."

"I'm not a loose person," Isabel said. She started swacking through the grass to find her ball.

Irons made no effort to look for his. "My guess is you're an only child," he said. "And an orphan now, too." She squinted up at him briefly, without expression, then resumed her search.

"Am I right?" he persisted. "If it makes any difference, my mom and dad were in that plane that blew up over Scotland."

She stopped moving around. "Really?"

"Would I invent such a thing?"

She frowned. "Sorry," she said. "About your parents," she added hastily.

"But not about being a windchill. Okay." He nodded at her. "Thanks, anyway, for the expression of sympathy. Which we both know sounds stilted, automatic, superficial, and completely useless." He smiled.

In spite of her anger, she smiled back. "That's a good way of putting it."

"So how about seeing if you can get anything that isn't superficial and useless from us deep-down-sensitive-beneath-a-rough-exterior guys, seeing that we are here today?"

She was searching again. "Where the hell *is* my ball?"

"I'm standing on it with my left foot."

She jerked her head up.

"But it's all right because with my right foot I'm standing on mine. Don't worry, we can improve our lies."

"The others have already hit. Out of turn."

"I told them to go ahead with a secret brother-hood hand signal," Irons said.

"So you could soften me up over here in the tough grass?"

"Exactly. Look, here's all we want you to think about—in all those other foursomes you've played in, why haven't you scattered your dad's remains? And can we be any different, so that today you can finally unload that pack?"

With that he stepped off both balls. They

were nicked with spike marks, and embedded deep. Irons bent and picked his up, then set it carefully on a tee of grass he cropped with his hand. After a moment, Isabel did the same.

"I'm away," he said, and quickly lifted a high five-iron shot down the fairway. He waited until she had smacked a longer three-iron, then walked off ahead of her.

"And now I guess I'm supposed to do all that thinking," she said in a low voice. She tried to say it with a scoff, but the scoff didn't really come.

5.

THE twelfth hole was a long par three with a large, flat green thirty feet below the level of the tee. The boys were off first. Flipper's five-iron held on the back edge, forty feet to the left of the cup, while Irons shanked a six-iron short and far right. Jackson, appraising the green and waggling his club with his persistent good cheer, plopped his ball tight to the pin. He twirled his five-iron as if it were a baton and whistled for himself.

Isabel took her three-iron from her bag.

"What are you hitting?" said Flipper.

She looked back at him, then at the others. "A three," she said, looking a little uncomfortable. "I tee it up high so I get under it, cut the distance, get some loft so maybe it will bite the green." She shrugged. "If I do it just right, it flies more like a five-iron."

Flipper pulled a club from his bag and held it out. "Why not just *use* a five, then?"

Before Isabel decided what to say, Irons and Jackson howled.

"It must be love!" Irons crowed.

"I think Flip just *proposed!*"

Flipper blushed and shot them a scowl. Irons said to Isabel, "See, he never, ever lets anybody use one of those nineteen or twenty-two or whatever absurd number of sticks he carries in that uptown bag of his. We've been playing with him for four years and he won't let us even *heft* one."

"This," Jackson said with reverence, "is a major step of human evolution we are witnessing."

Flipper pretended to ignore them. He gave the five-iron a shake, keeping his eyes on Isabel. "You're welcome to try with this," he said. "Unless you feel safer with your three."

"Safer!" said Jackson. "Isabel, I wouldn't swing with that club unless you're sure he's protected."

Now Isabel blushed. But she took the club from Flipper and put her three-iron back in her bag. The boys watched with expectant silence through two practice swings.

She stepped up to her ball. Without looking

up, she said, "If I hit a bad one, it's all your fault, Flipper."

"She called you by an endearment," Jackson whispered loudly.

Isabel did *not* hit a bad one. Flying high and straight, her ball dropped on the front lip of the green, bounced once, and settled twenty feet downhill from the cup.

It seemed as if the three boys had held their breath; they burst out at once with cheers. Isabel did not acknowledge them right away. She slowly brought Flipper's iron down from her follow-through, gave it an appreciative look, then walked over and returned it.

"Great club," she said to Flipper with a smile. "Thanks."

Flipper nodded, not meeting her eyes, and put the iron back into his bag.

On the fairway this time, Isabel found herself walking once more with Jackson.

"So," he said brightly, "are you alone now?"

She stopped and looked at him coldly. He seemed not to notice, holding his easy, expectant smile. After a moment, she walked on. "I haven't been thinking of it that way before today," she said, head down. "But—yes, I'm

145

alone. My mother died of lupus when I was five. So, without my father—yes, I'm an orphan now."

"Well, hey," said Jackson, "I'm an orphan, too!" *He* sounded as if they had just discovered they had the same birthday.

Isabel looked shocked. "*You* are? But—"

Jackson laughed. "Quite a few people qualify, you know. Like Irons, too. Nothing very exclusive about it."

"But—but you're so chipper!" It sounded like a reproach.

He smiled. "Nothing crippling about it, either. I mean, *they're* dead, but you stay who you are."

She looked doubtful. "I suppose," she said. "Eventually."

They stopped and waited for Irons to chip from the woods, over the green to the left rough. When they were walking again, Jackson said, "Actually, there's nothing 'eventual' about it—you stay yourself all along. You don't have to *do* anything. Just keep moving." He thought for a moment. "It's not a condition that hangs on you forever, like Flipper's arm."

Isabel said nothing. They paused again, as Irons swung disgustedly at his ball and hit a beautiful shot to within ten feet of the hole.

Flipper was ready, and whacked his long putt. It stopped four feet short.

Now Isabel was away. She studied the line of her putt, stood over the ball, and stroked it. She watched in evident surprise as it held a good line, reached the cup, and lipped out, to rest a foot uphill.

"Nice ball," Jackson said, close behind her. She turned, looking startled that he had stayed close.

He smiled. "Dump the ashes, Isabel."

"What did you say?"

"Dump the ashes. Choose a spot that's okay, and let 'em go."

"You can't tell me . . ."

"Sssh," he said with a finger to his lips. He pointed past her. She turned in time to see Irons lining up his ten-footer. He sank it, and tried to act as if nothing extraordinary had happened. Flipper said something caustic to him, then sank his own.

Isabel turned back to Jackson. She tried to summon her previous outrage, but it wouldn't quite come, though she said once more, "You have no right—"

"Maybe not," he said, "but I do have a feeling.

All of us do, the same one. You think you're waiting to find the perfect place to do it, the perfect moment and all that." He shook his head. "But you must know by now that's not what it's about. Okay, it's cool you decided to scatter his remains on a place he liked. Fine. You're here. You have the ashes. So scatter them, already. The longer you wait, the more you're going to fool yourself into believing you're really carrying your *dad* around, in that pack you wear like some kind of punishment."

Before Isabel could sputter a response, Jackson said, "Excuse me a minute," and walked to his ball. He tapped his two-foot putt into the center of the hole. Then he laid his putter on the green, raised his hands, and beckoned to Irons and Flipper. He said, "Let's have it, dudes."

Isabel watched blankly as Irons and Flipper began to circle him, crouching low, flapping their arms, and uttering falsetto peeps.

Jackson, arms crossed, looked over at her haughtily. "Come on," he said. "Everyone has to do it."

"Do *what?*"

"The birdie dance," Irons said, between sharp peeps. "He shot a birdie, so . . ."

Uncertainly Isabel put her putter down and

walked over. She waited for an opening between Irons and Flipper, then joined the circle.

"Make yourself smaller," Jackson said. "And I don't hear any peeping."

Isabel crouched lower. And peeped.

Jackson cupped one ear with a hand. She peeped more loudly.

"Don't worry," Irons whispered. "It's only for a minute."

"Yeah," said Flipper. "You just have to let go and do it."

"So I hear," said Isabel.

"No talking!" said Jackson sternly. "Do birdies talk? No, they do not. Birdies *peep*."

They *peeped*.

6.

ON the tee of the fifteenth, Irons handed Isabel his driver. "You really ought to air one out here. Use this. And maybe you should hit this drive without your pack."

He said it casually. Isabel quickly looked at the three of them. Jackson was using the tip of a tee to pick dirt from the grooves of his club. Flipper had just washed his ball and was drying it on a yellow towel attached to his bag. No one looked as if anything momentous was in the offing.

"Yes, we know," Irons said. "You've probably played twenty rounds and hit every shot out from under that thing." He shrugged, then squinted down the long fairway stretching without visible end in the sunlight. "But this is *this* hole, *this* shot. And it's stupid, stupid *golf* to keep it on."

Isabel looked at him, looked at the other two. They all watched her now. She held back a sigh and said, "Well, my father didn't teach me to play stupid golf." Then she slipped her arms out of the pack's straps and slung the weight to the ground.

"Hey, miracle diet!" Jackson said. "Lose five pounds on one par five!"

Flipper said only, "Give it a rip, Isabel."

She took six practice swings, looking slightly uncomfortable.

"Okay," she said. "Sorry."

She drew back too far on her backswing, and whipped too hard through impact. The ball streaked away like a sparrow chased by a falcon, staying low and darting into a sharp hook. It disappeared beneath trees two hundred yards away.

She stomped once with a curse, then turned to the boys. "I know what I did wrong!" she said almost eagerly. "I know. I can fix it, I can fix it for the next drive, really!"

The boys smiled. Isabel jigged impatiently. "I *will*," she said.

"We don't doubt it," said Irons.

Isabel caught Flipper looking down beside her, and followed his eyes to her pack on the ground. "Oh," she said. The boys waited. She looked from the pack to them, back at the pack, back to them. "Do you think—I mean, is it okay—"

"What do you think, boys?" said Jackson. The three of them exchanged thoughtful frowns.

"I don't know," said Flipper doubtfully. "She started with the pack on, we adjusted our game to the way she played with the pack on . . . seems a lot to ask us to change everything now. Isn't there something written about fixed accessories assuming permanent status after nine holes?"

"We need a ruling, maybe," said Jackson.

Irons shook his head. "It's not a *fixed* accessory," he said. "It's a *detachable* accessory. Or at least I *think* it is."

"Yeah," said Jackson. "I get what you mean." He looked skeptically at the pack on the ground. "Probably detachability needs to be fully demonstrated. Sustained, like."

Flipper said, "Okay. I can go with that. *If*"— he held up a finger—"*If* it is clearly shown that the detachment of the accessory is not just kind of frivolous."

"If the detachment were shown to be a progressive step toward some kind of further detachment, perhaps even a *resolution,* would that suffice?" said Irons.

Flipper considered, then nodded.

Jackson said, "I can accept that."

Isabel picked up the pack. "No," she said. "Your little game is what's frivolous—"

"You're the one playing a little game, Isabel," Irons said, shaking his head. "The rest of us are playing golf. You do what you want. But get out of the way now so we can hit."

7.

THE par five made for long treks. Isabel and Flipper walked together.

Flipper, nervous, said, "All that stuff back a while with the five-iron—"

"Don't worry," she said tersely. "You're not committed."

He seemed stung. Isabel relented a bit. "Look, you were nice to me. Thanks. That's all."

He thought for a second. He said, "What about what we said together on the last tee? We were being nice to you then, too."

She sighed, and shifted the pack on her back. "Were you?"

"I guess it's a lot easier to take a club for one shot than to take a little friendship."

"Oh, that's profound." But after only a moment she sighed again and said, "Maybe it's partly the funeral jive I'm trying to get away from."

"Was it bad?" Flipper said.

"It was grotesque." She shook her head. "The bats who ran the show threw what was nothing more than a party in honor *not* of my father but in honor of *death*. They set up his coffin, open, in the middle of this fake-elegant room and let all of my relatives run wild, getting wasted on tranquilizers because the whole thing was *so* stressful for them, gathering over the body all evening and talking in fake-grim voices about how good he looked. Good! He was dead!"

"A party with a corpse instead of a band."

Isabel looked at him appreciatively. "Exactly!"

Flipper said, "And I bet you didn't go over and look."

"Right. I did *not*. I had seen him alive. That—" she stopped short, turned pale.

Flipper hesitated, and finally asked, "Did you find him? After he died?"

She nodded, still pale.

"So you'd seen him dead already," Flipper said. "I'm sorry, Isabel. That must have been rougher than anything could be."

She tried to shrug. It didn't work. A moment later she said, "He was in a chair when I came into the house. He looked asleep. It took me a few minutes, talking to him like a fool, just babbling on, before I realized. Then it suddenly felt like it was happening to somebody else. I even heard my own voice as it kept on babbling. Didn't recognize it. I thought, *Why doesn't that stupid person shut UP?*"

"What did you do?"

"Oh, just what a good citizen does when she finds a dead body. Called 911. Didn't touch anything. Opened the door for the ambulance guys and the cops. I was in the kitchen talking to the police when the medical people took him out to the ambulance and away. I didn't even see him leave." She held her voice for a moment. "I never saw him again."

"Well," said Flipper, "nobody did, right? I mean, he was dead. You didn't really even see him when you found him in the chair. Not *him,* really." She said nothing; he said, "Right?"

"All of you three are pretty philosophical about my dad's death, you know that? Maybe it's harder when it happens to you." She looked at him, but said nothing more for the rest of the hole. But when they arrived at her ball, she took her backpack off to swing, after only a slight hesitation.

8.

SHE hit a three-iron too fat, but still in the fairway. She and Flipper moved twenty feet farther to his ball. He made no move to take a shot; instead, he was frowning as he obviously considered whatever difficult thing came next to say.

Isabel cut off his thoughts. "Play," she said. Flipper looked up at her. She said coldly, "No more talking from me. I haven't talked this much—"

"—since the big fellow died," came the voice of Jackson close by. Isabel spun to look behind her. "Don't look so angry," he said with a grin. He held up an eight-iron for them to see. "I'm not spying. While you two were arguing about whether to go to Hawaii or Disney World on the honeymoon, I skulled a shot into these trees."

"You could have hollered," said Flipper.

"You're right," Jackson said easily. "I could

have." He was swishing his club through the rough, with one hand holding it loosely.

Flipper said, "The trees are over there, Jackson, or didn't you notice?"

"Thanks, Flip, I did. And thanks also for the offer to help me look for my ball." He continued to rake lightly through the high grass. "But, see, if we got serious about this, we might actually find the little sucker. And it would probably be smack behind a tree trunk or stuck between two roots." He poked at a tuft. "This way, after an appropriate expenditure of time, I can give up and take a sweet drop." He stopped, looked across the fairway to where Irons stood watching, and raised his arms in a big shrug of helplessness. Irons made a wave of disgust.

Jackson teed up a new ball on a pedestal of grass, looked up the fairway, and swooped a high, curving shot of perhaps eighty yards. "Perfect," he said. "Your turn, Flip."

Flipper, looking flustered, hurried his swing and hit a long hook that curled out of their sight.

"Hey, I think you caught the water over that way, Flip," Jackson said helpfully.

Flipper stomped off without a word.

9.

ON the seventeenth tee the boys arrived first, put their bags down, and sat on them.

Isabel walked up. "What's this?" She remained upright.

"Group therapy," said Jackson.

"An ambush," said Flipper.

"A friendly but firm chat, is all," said Irons. "Have a seat."

Isabel lowered her bag and the backpack in her other hand, but stood. Slowly, warily, she checked the gaze of each boy. "Okay," she said, "let's hear it."

"Only two holes left," Irons said. "Time we came up with the plan for how you are going to distribute your father's ashes."

She shook her head with a smile of disbelief. "Oh, yeah? Why?"

"Because today's the day," said Irons. "A month is long enough. And it is doubtful you will ever

again find yourself in such a congenial, con-
cerned, intelligently balanced foursome."

"Is that so?"

Irons nodded. "It is. And here we find ourselves
narrowing the scope of sites for a dignified, appropriate dispersal—as judged, of course, entirely by
you. Please let us say that we do understand, as
much as we can, the sensitive issues involved for
you in letting go of your father's remains. Let us
emphasize, too: That isn't your father inside that
little backpack."

Isabel snapped, "You don't have any idea—"

But Flipper cut her off. "And even if it were
some, like, mystical ghost of your dad in there,
and you want to honor the link between him and
the game he loved—well, carrying him around a
golf course for a month must do the job, right? I
mean, a month!"

For a long moment of silence, Isabel looked at
the ground between her feet. Then she very delib-
erately sat on her bag. "The thing is," she said,
frowning at the ground, "it was *not* suicide."

The boys exchanged quick glances. Flipper
said, "Okay."

She looked up, and her focus found Flipper. "He was what they call bipolar. Manic-

depressive. Basically, big super-energetic high times, and bad, bad low-down blue times. But a few years ago, he started getting meds. Drugs."

"Lithium?" said Jackson. The others looked at him. "I listen to my Nirvana," he said.

"No," said Isabel. "Too many side effects. Instead, he took this complicated combination of pills—two antidepressants, two antianxiety drugs, a mood stabilizer to regulate the manic phase, a drug to cancel the soporific effects of *that* drug, and, finally, a tranquilizer in case all the other things freaked him out."

"Sheez," said Irons.

"So that's, like, what, eight pills a day?" said Jackson.

"Eighteen," Isabel said.

"Did he write it all down hour by hour or something?" said Flipper.

Isabel shook her head and sighed. "No. I wish he had—or I wish at least he'd had that attitude. Careful about it all. But"—she almost smiled—"he was kind of a cowboy about the drugs. My dad was very smart, *very* smart, and he figured since it was his body and his awareness, he could tell day by day what he needed. So he tended to improvise."

161

"Danger," said Irons.

"Death," said Flipper.

Isabel did not respond. "The tranquilizer was this kind of concentrated downer that apparently you don't *feel*—it doesn't make you woozy or anything. But it has big effects down deep." She sighed.

"He took too much of that," said Irons.

She nodded. "But not because he needed to tank out. See, he got frequent kidney stones."

"Ouch," said Jackson. "Had one. Wanted to die." He put his hand over his mouth. "Oops."

Isabel gave him a half-smile. "It's okay. The autopsy showed my dad had a stone between his kidney and his bladder. That's the tiny tube, see, the one the stone rips up, the one that spasms." She sighed. "Evidently, my dad decided he could maybe relax those tubes or something by taking a bunch of his tranks." She gave a small shrug, and in a smaller voice said, "He took too many."

Silence. Irons said, "Was too many a lot?"

Isabel waited, then shook her head. "Not so many," she said. "As I said, they were stronger than they felt."

They sat in silence for a minute or more. Finally, Jackson pointed to the backpack and said, "And you have to carry that *thing* around until you feel you can let go of 'him' forever."

Isabel said nothing. Neither did the boys. Then, after a few moments, she said, in a smaller voice, "It's all I have."

"Then you don't have much, do you?" said Irons. "A box of junk that keeps you from taking a decent swing while you 'honor' him by playing around on his golf course."

Isabel was crimson. "Listen," she said through gritted teeth, "I *told* you it's all I *have*."

"Bullshit," said Flipper. He looked surprised at himself for a second, then went on more softly. "You've got a lot more than that left. Check it out every time you swing a club."

Isabel said nothing. They watched her think for long moments. It was silent except for some birdsong and the distant sounds of occasional golf shots on other fairways.

"Okay," Irons said at last, "the seventeenth offers mostly water for the dispersal of remains— it's a par three over a pond and a creek. Did your father catch the water often?"

Isabel shook her head.

"Then I suggest that scattering the ashes over the drink would not be appropriate. Isabel?"

She shook her head.

"Very well," said Irons. "That leaves us the final hole, the par-five eighteenth, a real bear because of the four huge sand traps around the green, each of them ready to suck in a three-wood shot that lands too hot." He narrowed his eyes at Isabel. "Now, answer carefully. Did your father, by any chance, have a tendency to hit into bunkers?"

Isabel looked at him. "Yes," she said. "Yes, he did. It was if he aimed at sand instead of at the green."

Irons leaned back, holding his palms up and looking at the other two boys. "There we have it," he said.

"Have what?" said Isabel.

"Sand," said Irons.

"Sand?" said Jackson.

Isabel looked at Irons. "You mean—you're saying I should—"

"Scatter," said Irons.

"—scatter these in a sand trap at the eighteenth green?"

Irons looked at Jackson and Flipper. Small nods passed between them. "Sounds good to us," said Irons. They stood, flashing that-takes-care-of-*that* grins.

Isabel looked at the boys. As they watched, *her* face seemed to turn both soft and tense, innocent and overwise; tears pushed their way into the corners of her eyes, waiting.

The boys stared back, self-congratulatory smiles gone. As a silence held them all, Irons, Flipper, and Jackson began to look as if they suddenly realized they might have fixed nothing.

Flipper got there first. "We figured out what to do with the *ashes*," he said, still looking at Isabel. He smiled tentatively, "But we're forgetting. It's not *about* the ashes, is it?"

Isabel held his eyes but made no move or sound.

"Oh, man," Jackson said miserably.

"It's about Isabel," Irons said. "It's about you."

Isabel hunched her shoulders in a shrug. After another minute of silence all around, she stood up. "No," she said. "No, I don't think it's about me anymore. I thought it was about my father, but it wasn't. I did not think it was about me, but I guess it was." She sighed again. "But now it really *is* about just a box of ashes."

Another silence. But Irons broke it quickly. "Well," he said, pulling an iron from his bag, "you've got two holes, Isabel. We'll just play golf, and leave it to you."

10.

THE four of them played the seventeenth mechanically, with tunnel vision, without speaking. The eighteenth went the same way, until the time came for approach shots to the green. Before hitting, each looked nervously at the others. The plea was clear in the eyes: *Please keep it out of the traps.*

The pleas evidently worked; all four balls ended up on the green. Still, without speaking, the four of them putted out. Then they stepped off the green, and Flipper spoke to Isabel. "We'll just wait wherever you want us to," he said. "Maybe under the trees over there? You can"— he waved his hand at the bunkers—"well, there are trap rakes at each one, so . . ."

The boys started to move away.

"Wait," said Isabel.

They stopped, and looked at her. She picked

up the backpack, unfastened the clasp, and pulled out a square black box. She took two steps, turned her back to the boys. They heard cardboard rip. They saw her neck stiffen. She looked away, raised her face upward for a moment.

Over her shoulder she glanced at them again. Then she walked to the closest trap, stepped down into the sand, and crunched out to the middle. Holding the box in both hands, she tilted it and shook, until a small stream of textured gray dust spilled out, making a cone on the sand. Isabel tipped the box back. The flow of ashes stopped.

She walked out of that bunker and into the middle of the next, where she repeated the ritual with the box and the stream of ashes and the cone. Then she did it twice more. As she stepped out of the fourth trap, she flung the box away, empty.

Without looking at the waiting boys, Isabel walked by the bunkers and picked up the small aluminum trap rake on the edge of each. She climbed the incline back to the level of the green, and stood before the boys.

She looked each one in the eyes with a small smile, and handed him a rake. The fourth she held on to.

They watched her. She kept her slight smile, and nodded. "Pick a pile," she said.

Hesitantly, the boys spread out, and stepped into the sand traps, glancing frequently at Isabel, who had strode out into the fourth trap and stood with her rake poised over the cone of ashes at her feet.

At last, they all took a similar stance. No one moved. The boys watched Isabel.

"Well?" she said.

"We're waiting," Jackson said, "for you to tell us who's away."

Isabel laughed. "Nobody's away now," she said. "This we do as a foursome. Got it?"

They all bent and began to rake.